THE WORLD AT THE EDGE OF SPACE

PERSEUS GATE – EPISODE 2

By M. D. Cooper

SPECIAL THANKS

Just in Time (JIT) & Beta Reads

Lisa L. Richman
Scott Reid
Kristina Able
David Wilson

Cover Art by Andrew Dobell
Editing by Tee Ayer

TABLE OF CONTENTS

FOREWORD

I'm having a blast writing these Perseus Gate books, and I sincerely hope they are fun reads for you. I feel like I'm channeling my love of Farscape into them, and that's a great thing.

In this episode, the crew must begin their journey across Orion Space to the Inner Stars, and then to New Canaan, deep within the Transcend. They're looking at twenty years of travel—if they can get a dark layer map, and supplies.

It's going to be a wild ride getting back home, one that will send the crew of *Sabrina* down some rabbit holes on the far side of space.

M. D. Cooper

SABRINA'S CREW

Cargo – Ship's Captain
Cheeky – Pilot
Erin – AI embedded in Nance
Finaeus – Passenger
Jessica – First Mate
Hank – AI embedded in Cargo
Iris – AI embedded in Jessica
Nance – Bio/Engineer
Piya – AI embedded in Cheeky
Sabrina – Ship's AI
Trevor – Supercargo and muscle

NOTE: When *Sabrina* is italicized, it refers to the ship, but if Sabrina is not italicized, it refers to the AI. Yes, this would be much simpler if the ship and AI did not share the same name, but you try telling that to Sabrina!

Just so you stay on her good side, never call the ship "**the** *Sabrina*"; it really gets on her last synthetic neuron.

MAPS

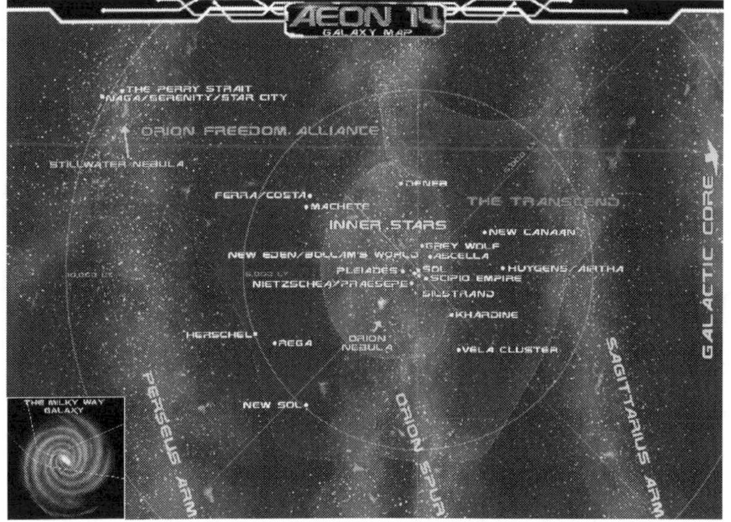
AEON 14
GALAXY MAP
THE PERRY STRAIT
NAGA/SERENITY/STAR CITY
ORION FREEDOM ALLIANCE
STILLWATER NEBULA
FERRA/COSTA
MACHETE
DENEB
THE TRANSCEND
INNER STARS
NEW CANAAN
GREY WOLF
NEW EDEN/BOLLAM'S WORLD
ASCELLA
PLEIADES
SOL
HUYGENS/AIRTHA
NIETZSCHEA/PRAESEPE
SCIPIO EMPIRE
SILSTRAND
KHARDINE
HERSCHEL
REGA
ORION NEBULA
VELA CLUSTER
NEW SOL
THE MILKY WAY GALAXY
PERSEUS ARM
ORION SPUR
SAGITTARIUS ARM
GALACTIC CORE

AWAKEN

STELLAR DATE: 07.22.8938 (Adjusted Years)
LOCATION: *Sabrina*, Outside Naga's Heliopause
REGION: Perseus Arm of the Milky Way Galaxy

Consciousness returned to Cheeky in slow, unsteady increments.

At first it felt as though she was surrounded by a nimbus glow and fear set in instantly.

I'm dead. Fuck, I'm dead!

There was no answer to her cry. The glow didn't change, and Cheeky tried to reach Piya.

<Hello? Piya? Are you there? Are we in the black hole? Is this what happens when you get compressed down to nothing?>

Piya didn't respond, but Cheeky felt her Link re-initialize and her neural enhancements come online. She *was* alive, surely neural enhancements didn't persist into the afterlife.

An ear-splitting screech assaulted Cheeky and she screamed.

"Cheeky, can you hear me?" a voice said as the screech began to fade.

Cheeky realized she still had a mouth and it seemed to work, though it was dry, and her tongue felt stiff.

"Y-yes…"

"Good! That means your new ears are working. Your eyes are open, but you probably can't see yet. Give it another couple of minutes while your visual implants calibrate."

"Is that you, Jessica?"

"Yup!" Jessica replied brightly. "We've been taking shifts with you, waiting for you to awake. Looks like I won the lotto."

"Are we…is *Sabrina* OK? I remember seeing a huge fight—right before…"

"Yes," Jessica said, confirming Cheeky's memory. "We made it. We *all* made it—sorta."

"Where's Piya, then?" Cheeky asked. "And what do you mean about 'sorta'?"

"Piya wrote herself into static storage, so she's safe. You took a lot of radiation damage out there, and we had to restore parts of your organic brain before we could pull her out. Your vision centers were the worst. The medbay's autodoc replaced all of that with artificial matrices for now."

Cheeky took a deep breath. She remembered passing over the mining ring, seeing the searingly-bright accretion disks of the orbiting black holes, the baleful light of the Grey Wolf Star. The heat. So much heat.

"And the 'sorta'?" she asked after a moment's contemplation.

"Well, we jumped through the gate! Yay! Go us, and all that. Finaeus and Nance got a mirror made in time—by some truly serendipitous work on Nance's part from what I can tell—but something went wrong. We're a ways from home."

Cheeky chuckled, the movement welcome, but painful at the same time. "If we're on *Sabrina*, then I'm home."

<*Thanks for the sentiment,*> Sabrina said.

"Sabs!" Cheeky cried out. "Are you OK? Did you get hurt?"

<*No, my new shields kept me safe. I'm an armored bee. I zip about, impregnable, impossible to hurt, but beware, my sting is deadly.*>

"Glad to see you're still rolling with the metaphors," Cheeky said with a smile, feeling her cheeks stretch differently than she was accustomed to. "I have artificial skin, don't I?"

"Yeah," Jessica replied and Cheeky could hear the smile in her voice. "Looks good on you too."

"Don't get any ideas," Cheeky replied. "I like my natural stuff. Don't think you're going to make me all plastic like you."

"It'd be fun!" Jessica laughed. "We could be twins!"

"Wait, stop changing the subject. What happened after we jumped? Are we coming into New Canaan now?"

"I didn't change the subject, you did," Jessica said, admonishing in both her tone and gaze.

<She's right, you did,> Sabrina added. *<Well, I guess I kinda jumped in and distracted you.>*

"Sooo…"

"Well, I assume you know of the Perseus Arm…"

"Of what? The Milky Way *Galaxy*?!"

"Yes," Jessica said, and Cheeky could hear the grin in her voice."

"Jessica! You better be kidding!"

OBSERVING NAGA

STELLAR DATE: 08.19.8938 (Adjusted Years)
LOCATION: *Sabrina*, Outside Naga's Heliopause
REGION: Perseus Arm of the Milky Way Galaxy

"Seriously?" Cheeky asked from the pilot's console on the bridge. "Who names their system 'Naga' anyway. Just sounds like some awful place full of complainers and whiners or something."

Jessica shrugged. "Maybe it is—or maybe it means something like 'delicious fish' to the locals."

"Doubtful," Cargo said. "Place looks light on the...well... everything. I don't think there's anything delightful about it."

Jessica had to agree. From what their passive scans of the system had picked up, there was one—marginally—terraformed world, a few dozen space stations, and a couple of habs on the moons around one of the jovian worlds.

Radio traffic and energy output substantiated an estimate of less than one million inhabitants.

"They should still have supplies, and we can scoop deuterium and helium-3 off their star, or one of the jovian planets," Finaeus said.

"Plus, there's nothing else around for at least ten light years. I don't fancy dumping into the dark layer without any maps," Cheeky added with a glance back at Finaeus. "The jump to get here was terrifying enough as it was."

Jessica noted a softness in Cheeky's expression as she glanced at the ancient terraformer. As the pilot turned back to her console, her eyes caught Jessica's.

<*What?*> Cheeky asked privately, her mental tone a touch defensive.

<*What, what?*> Jessica replied. <*Just looking at you, is all.*>

<*You think—*> Cheeky began to say, but Jessica interrupted her.

<*Cheeks, we're a billion kilometers from home, probably stuck together on this ship for another two decades. If you want to taste ancient man to see how salty he is, that's fine by me.*> She drew a circle in the air around herself and winked. <*This is a zero-judgment zone here.*>

Cheeky gave a soft chuckle and then winced as she turned back to her console.

<*That taste may have to wait till all my bits and pieces stop hurting. Did you ache this much after you got your skin burned off back in Victoria?*>

Jessica's mind flashed back to that fight in the deep black at the edge of the Kapteyn's Star System. She had been part of a fighter squadron flying in the older ARC-5 models—though they had been new at the time. The enemy had been a trio of Sirian scout ships sent to probe the Victoria colony for weaknesses

One of the enemy ships had detonated their reactors rather than be captured, and Jessica's fighter had been close. Too close. It had taken days for the S&R crews to find her, and when they did she had been in rough shape.

She looked down at her hand, rubbing her purple-hued fingers together. That was when she had received her first artificial skin—something necessary to replace her long-gone natural skin, and to seal her weakened body off from infection.

<*Yeah, Cheeks, I ached all over, and in places that I didn't even know you could ache—for a month at least. Regrowing organs in place has a way of doing that.*>

<*Aches I can handle, it's the nails constantly being driven into my skull that are the problem. Piya says it's just my brain adjusting its blood flow requirements after the reconstruction…but it feels like it's tearing itself apart up there,*> Cheeky replied.

<*Yeah, I remember that, it was the pits. But it passes. You'll be back to fucking everything in sight in no time.*>

Cheeky passed a mental smile over the Link. <*Not a lot to fuck on board right now. Just Finaeus and Cargo—you've been off the menu for years now.*>

<*Yeah…Monogamous J-doll, that's me,*> Jessica chuckled. <*But don't forget Nance. You and she have had some flings in the past.*>

<*Jessica! Too soon. She just lost Thompson. Nance really thought they had a real thing going on,*> Cheeky said, apparently aghast at the suggestion.

<*Yeah,* **she** *thought that, but we all knew he had no intention of ever settling down with her.*>

<*Yeah, you and I know that,*> Cheeky replied. <*But our sweet little Nance was hell-bent on domesticating that giant asshole.*>

<*Cheeky! Gross! Careful with the visuals!*>

"Sabrina," Cargo asked, his voice breaking into Jessica and Cheeky's private conversation. "Any luck on faking an ident?"

<*Iris is sneaking a look at their logs in a nearby beacon. She's better at that sort of thing than I am,*> Sabrina replied on the general shipnet.

<*It's slow going,*> Iris said. <*Beacon is a light-minute out. I'm sending discreet packets through a small relay drone I dropped off. I should get…yes, got the logs from when the beacon was first deployed. Gee, just seventy years ago.*>

"Was it a replacement?" Cargo asked.

<*Hard to say,*> Iris replied. <*It's codes are close to, but subtly different than the Transcend's. But if I had to hazard a guess I'd say it was part of the original deployment.*>

"Seventy years," Jessica said, whistling. "Then we really are close to the edge."

<*Well, there are no radio signals coming in from any stars toward the galactic rim,*> Sabrina said, a strangely-wistful tone in her mental voice.

"What's got you so dreamy, Sabs?" Cheeky asked.

<Well, how often do you get to the edge of known space?> Sabrina asked. *<Don't you just want to turn toward the rim and keep flying to see what's out there?>*

"No," Cargo responded.

"Not especially," Jessica added.

"Been there, done that," Finaeus chuckled. "It can be fun, but really, it's just rocks and stars and balls of gas. They all start to look the same after a while."

"That can't be how you feel about it," Cheeky said. "I bet you've seen some amazing things out there. Like…what's the weirdest animal you ever encountered?"

Finaeus put a hand to his chin. "Hmmmm…there aren't as many extra-terrestrial lifeforms that one would consider to be 'animals' as you'd think. We *made* most of the animals that you find on the FGT terraformed worlds—even the really weird stuff like the flying pigs on Sardonis in the Aldebaran system. Most of the crazy things are just adaptations of things from Earth, or Earth's far past—stuff that we adjusted to be suited to the planets after terraforming was done."

"Yeah, but there *are* alien lifeforms on some worlds. Things that existed before the FGT showed up and started terraforming," Cargo said.

"Yeah, we did encounter worlds that already had life. Mostly the worst things that we hit were plants that were a bit more mobile than we would have preferred—or right-handed biology. That stuff is a real pain in the ass to deal with."

"Right handed biology?" Cheeky asked.

Finaeus chuckled. "Where's Nance when you need her? She'd know about this stuff. On Earth, life evolved using what are called left-handed amino acids. We know now that it was a quirk of the supernova that caused the Sol System to form that made them so. However, on many other worlds, right-handed amino acids were prevalent, and life formed from those."

"What's the big deal about that?" Cargo asked, appearing genuinely curious.

"Right-handed biology might as well be silicon-based as far as humans are concerned. If you encountered a right-handed plant and tried to eat it, it wouldn't be able to interact with your body. It would be about as nutritious as sand—and don't even get me started on the places where life evolved using amino acids *and* sugars. Those places are nuts."

"Nuts, how?" Cheeky asked.

"Well, one of them had trees with leaves that appeared to be crystalline; sharp too, could cut you wide open. Then there was this one low-*g* world—a super-Earth, so the thing was huge—where the surface of the planet was covered in kilometers of this weird foamy stuff. It wasn't a fungus or anything analogous to Terran life.

"Actually, that's where the weirdest animal was from too!"

"Oh yeah?" Cargo asked. "What was it?"

"Well, it was kinda disgusting. It was basically a giant tick-looking thing that had a huge airbag on its back. It would float along, above the foamy surface of the world, and when it found some place that had its version of food, it would plop down, dig in and absorb it all. It wouldn't have been so bad if they weren't almost a kilometer across, and thought our ships were great snacks—we spent half our time avoiding the things."

Cheeky gave a convulsive shiver, and Jessica found herself in agreement with the sentiment. A kilometer-sized tick trying to eat a ship was the stuff of nightmares.

"Seriously?" Cargo laughed. "That thing sounds hilarious, not dangerous. What could it do to a ship anyway? You could just shoot your way out."

"Yeah." Finaeus nodded in agreement. "But then who's gonna clean the ship. Not me, that's for sure."

<*This is not my favorite conversation we've ever had,*> Sabrina said, her tone wavering. <*I already know that there are monsters in the dark layer, I didn't need to know that there are planets with things big enough to eat me.*>

"Sera told you guys about those, did she?" Finaeus asked. "For someone running The Hand, she's not so good about keeping secrets."

<*I got it!*> Iris announced. <*I found a ship that has a really close profile to ours. I can alter their logs to make us match. It's from a long way off too, so they won't be able to crosscheck our registry for months.*>

"Then what's our new name?" Cargo asked.

<*Sorry, Sabrina, you're going to hate this,*> Iris warned. <*We're now the* Matron Tulip.>

<*Oh no, oh stars no. Iris, find a different ship. Any ship, I'd rather be the* Pooping Dingo *than the* Matron Tulip*!*>

<*Sorry, Sabrina, these folks don't get a lot of traffic, and what they do get is just the same few interstellar haulers that pass through on regular runs. I need something to connect to. Our story gets really weak if* ***everything*** *about us is a fiction,*> Iris replied.

"What about crew?" Cargo asked. "Do we need to take on new personas?"

<*No. I'll flag a sale of the ship in our records and give us some sort of backstory,*> Iris said. <*Finaeus gave me enough data from what he has about Orion to cobble something together.*>

"It's not a lot, but it's some worlds, customs, and stuff that we can use if anyone enquires about where we're all from," Finaeus said.

"You're going to have to stay on the ship, though," Jessica said to Finaeus. "You're a well-known figure."

"Jessica, seriously, you tracked me half-way across the Inner Stars before catching up with me. I know how to blend in."

"Just this once," Cargo said with a note of finality in his voice. "We need to limit variables as much as possible this time out."

"Fine, Just be sure to pick up some good food," Finaeus said. "We're out of beef and lettuce. A good burger would go a long way when dealing with being cooped up in here."

"I'll add it to the grocery list," Cargo said while casting the older man a dour look.

"See that you do," Finaeus replied and walked off the bridge.

"Gee, he really wanted to get off the ship," Jessica said, staring after him.

"Can you blame him?" Cheeky asked. "We might not get to another station for weeks or months. Our little jaunt on Gisha Station wasn't exactly relaxing, I'll have you know."

"Well, at least you got off the ship," Jessica said with warm smile.

"Yeah, and then off the station, and almost into a black hole," Cheeky replied, her tone chilly.

Cargo chuckled, long and slow. "Well, then you certainly weren't bored."

Cheeky shot the captain a dark look before her shoulders slumped and she sighed. "Sorry, I didn't mean to snap. Getting a wicked headache."

<*You need to rest more,*> Piya said. <*Your body is building all sorts of new stuff right now.*>

"All sorts of new stuff?" Cheeky asked. "Is that code for *pretty much everything*?"

<*Yeah, I suppose,*> Piya said kindly. <*From what I see on your screen, we're still six hours from where we fake our dump in from the dark layer. Maybe you should get some rest.*>

Cheeky stood and nodded. "Yeah, that's a good idea. I'll catch a few winks before then, with your permission, Cargo."

"Of course." Cargo nodded. "Just be here thirty minutes before the maneuver."

"Thanks," Cheeky said as she left the bridge.

"Why don't you go get some downtime, too," Cargo said to Jessica. "We have our new name. From here it's just a matter of our virtual girls changing over all our ship's data. Same ole drill."

<*I happen to help out with all this too, you know,*> Hank said.

Cargo laughed. "Yeah, I know…I just felt lazy and didn't correct myself."

<*Wow, I feel so appreciated,*> Hank sighed.

"Your domestic issue aside, I think I'll take you up on that offer," Jessica said as she rose. "I'll see if Finaeus is up for a game of Snark. Trevor and Nance are in the middle of a grudge match, and will be busy for hours."

Finaeus poked his head back into the bridge and grinned. "Sure, why not. You need a good spanking."

"What? Are you just hanging out there eavesdropping?" Jessica asked.

"Of course, how else am I going to hear what you think of me while I'm not around."

"Get out of here, the both of you. But no spanking, Finaeus," Cargo said, cautioning her with a grin. "I saw the way Cheeky was looking at you. You're spoken for."

"I didn't mea—really? Think so?"

"Cargo made a funny!" Jessica laughed. "But he's right, Finaeus. Once Cheeky's mended, look out. You better make sure you're limber enough, old man."

"Oh, I'm limber enough." Finaeus grinned. "Did I ever mention the time when…"

<*Stars…if I send you an SOS, summon me for some sort of emergency,*> she said privately to Cargo.

The ship's captain just sent a mental laugh and waved her off the bridge.

RIGHT HAND TWIST

STELLAR DATE: 09.01.8938 (Adjusted Years)
LOCATION: *Sabrina*, Approaching Hermes Station
REGION: Naga System, Orion Freedom Alliance Space

Jessica examined the view on the bridge's main holotank. It rendered the planet Marsalla, and its largest moon, a near Luna-sized orb named Aresa. Their destination was highlighted on the display: a station named Hermes, which lay on the L1 point between the two celestial bodies.

However, no one was looking at the station; the planet Marsalla was far and away the most interesting object.

Its surface was covered with an apparent war between green and purple life. It was clearly visible across its continents and even within the oceans.

"So, not a terraformed world, then," Jessica said. "Just a conveniently-close-to-habitable one."

"That's a gem, is what that is," Finaeus added. "Look at it, almost Earth-sized, sixty, maybe sixty-five percent water. Oxygen/Nitrogen atmosphere. You can see FGT Model 18 carbon towers on the major continents, pumping CO2 into the atmosphere for all they're worth. Nice to see they're still using one of my designs even out here."

"But there's biomass down there," Cheeky said. "Life of some sort."

"Yeah," Finaeus said. "Sloppy. Shouldn't rush it like that."

"What do you mean?" Cargo asked. "It's going to take a while—decades at least—to make even parts of that planet livable. Doesn't seem like a rush to me."

Finaeus nodded. "Sure, but it should take longer. If you try to terraform a world that already has life without first sterilizing it, you won't like what you end up with. A middle-ground with terrestrial life and extraterrestrial life co-existing is not possible."

"Not true," Cheeky replied. "I've seen worlds where there was native life and stuff we brought there."

"Sorry," Finaeus said. "Poor choice of words. What I should have said is that it's not sustainable. If, by some miracle, one type of life doesn't obliterate the other, you end up with a subsumation and mutations."

"So why's the alien life purple?" Cheeky asked. "Is it a welcoming committee for Jessica?"

"Har har," Jessica said.

"Retinol, probably," Finaeus replied. "It's an alternate to chlorophyll. Simpler molecular structure. Most planets see retinol-utilizing life before chlorophyll comes along."

As he spoke, Nance walked onto the bridge, wearing her best hazsuit, with a clear spherical helmet tucked under one arm.

"Have you seen their decontamination protocols here?" she asked gesturing at the holodisplay, her voice raised in a combination of panic and professional indignation.

"Uh, yeah," Cheeky said. "They're all picky about going down to their planet, and bringing stuff up. Makes sense with what Finaeus was saying about mutations."

"All picky? All *picky*?" Nance exclaimed. "Their version of picky is a biophage waiting to happen! If this place isn't on the local 'no fly' list inside of the next half-century, I'll eat my hazsuit!"

Finaeus shrugged. "They may get some unpleasant outbreaks—depending on the type of life on that planet, but it's usually not the end of the world. Heh, see what I did there?"

"How come this sort of stuff—with mixed life forms—doesn't happen all the time?" Cargo asked. "There must be hundreds, maybe thousands of worlds that had native life.

Like Cheeky said, they're rare, but they're out there and don't seem to pose threats."

"That's because we sterilized the dangerous ones," Finaeus said with a devious smirk.

"What? You just wiped out entire worlds?" Cheeky asked. "That's…that's insane. How many did you destroy?"

Finaeus touched a hand to his chin and looked up at the overhead. "Hmm…at least seven-hundred by last count. Orion has probably done a bunch as well. Easily a thousand for sure."

"A thousand life-filled worlds?" Jessica asked. "Just gone?"

"Well, we just sterilized them, the worlds weren't gone. Some we had to do the whole system. Microbes are a persistent bunch. Keep in mind, most of these were worlds with little more than moss and lichen. Usually it's the fungus that we have to watch out for. That stuff is insidious."

<You sterilized the world with the flying tick things, right?> Sabrina asked.

"Actually, no. That one is still out there. It's life-type isn't a threat, and it's safe within the far reaches of the Transcend. But seriously, some of what we found could have wiped out humanity in a century. Interdicting the systems wouldn't have worked. Some asshole would have flown in eventually and then spread a phage that eventually killed everyone."

"Harsh," Cheeky said quietly. "But I get it."

"You didn't…kill any highly-evolved things—like primates—did you?" Jessica asked.

"Eliminate the competition sort of thing?" Finaeus asked. "I gotta tell you, we had some walloping debates over that issue through the years—even before the first ships left Sol. The public went over that one for decades. It was an interesting conundrum for the GSS."

As Finaeus chuckled to himself—clearly remembering the good ole days, Jessica filled in the term for everyone else.

"Generation Ship Service. A quasi-government agency that selected the crews for the original Future Generation Terraformers, and most of the colonist ships too."

"Why'd the call them the Generation Ships?" Cargo asked. "What with stasis and all."

"Didn't have that when we started," Finaeus said. "I can't tell you the amount of freezer burn I got from using cryopods. Those things are like a fucking lottery—in reverse."

"They also didn't expect old farts like Finaeus to just decide to live forever," Jessica added. "Even in my time, no one had anticipated that the FGT ships were still crewed with the original people sent out on them."

"What can I say," Finaeus grinned. "It hasn't been my time to go, yet."

"You didn't answer the question," Cheeky said.

"Which question?" Finaeus asked innocently.

"About killing off things like primates. Stuff that was close to becoming an intelligent sentient."

"Ah yes, well, it was tricky, you know. Everyone involved in the GSS and FGT believed in the preservation of the human race by spreading out. Eliminating potential competition is a great way to up our own odds of survival. However, an opposing point of view would argue that there *must* be other intelligent life out there somewhere, and if they see us exterminating everything, they might decide that *we're* the definition of unwanted competition. Our very actions could end up creating a self-fulfilling prophecy of our own doom."

"Sounds dramatic," Cargo said.

Jessica laughed. "Haven't you noticed? That's kinda Finaeus's thing."

Nance scowled. "You're really skirting the issue here."

<I'm interested in this too,> Sabrina said. *<I have less of an innate attachment to the concept of organic life evolving, but I do wonder if humans, or other AIs, quash new types of AI life as well.>*

"Oh gods, that's a whole different question," Finaeus said. "Regarding killing off primate-like things, we never had to test our resolve. We never found anything smarter than a cat out there. Sadly, so far, we're alone in the black."

<*In the Milky Way, at least,*> Iris added.

"Yes, yes," Finaeus nodded. "Other galaxies could be teeming with life—or there could be life on the far side of the galactic core, or even hiding in the larger nebulas. It's impossible to see what's out there without going to take a look."

"Which you have, haven't you?" Nance asked skeptically.

Finaeus shrugged. "Not the whole galaxy. But we've sent out probes that should have the job finished in ten to twenty-thousand years—depending on dark matter density in the galactic rim. The core will be lifeless, though. Everything within five kiloparsecs at least. Sagittarius A* makes certain of that."

<*Wouldn't that thing be a sight to see?*> Jessica asked Iris, referring to the supermassive black hole at the galaxy's core. <*Who knows, if we get the Transcend's longevity tech, maybe we will some day.*>

<*Well, I will,*> Iris said with a mischievous chuckle. <*Whether or not your organic self can even survive the radiation in the core is another question altogether. You might have to go full robo-doll.*>

<*Hey! Good point, though,*> Jessica replied.

"All very interesting stuff," Nance said. "However, as your ship's bio, I'm mandating that we practice full biocontainment procedures while we're at Hermes station. I don't want to leave this place and find out that we've got some fun new plankton growing on the bulkheads."

"Or inside our heads," Finaeus said with a somber nod. "Not that I would expect Orion to be so sloppy—they didn't build their empire by letting biophages run wild. Still, we're on their fringe, so caution is recommended."

"Speaking of which, we're fifteen minutes out from docking at Hermes station," Cheeky said. "They're sending a tug to bring us in the rest of the way."

Jessica glanced down at her console. "So far they haven't questioned our registry. Seems to be holding."

She turned back to the main holo where Hermes Station now filled the view. Hermes was the largest in the system, and as such the one they hoped to blend in on best. Though, even as the biggest in the system, it was barely noteworthy. Just a ring twenty kilometers in circumference, spinning around a central spire ten kilometers tall.

Even worse, there weren't a lot of ships present. Fewer than half of Hermes's berths were occupied, and the lanes in and out of the station contained little traffic.

They were going to stand out like sore thumbs.

"Everyone know their backstories?" Cargo asked to a chorus of yeses. "And you have your new tokens and ident data?"

"Yes, Dad." Cheeky chuckled. "Not our first-time faking ident, you know."

"Our first time where there's no safe haven to run to, though," Nance said. "Stars, we don't even know how to get to any other system, save blind jumps."

"Don't remind me," Cheeky groused.

"The station's pretty light on the regs," Jessica said. "What you'd expect for a bunch of scrappy types out on the fringe. If we're lucky it'll be filled with mostly live-and-let-live types. They do have a prohibition against public nudity…Cheeky… and only pulse pistols are allowed off-ship."

"They gonna inspect the bottle?" Nance asked.

"No word yet," Jessica replied, realizing that if Nance met the inspection team in a hazsuit it may arouse suspicion. "I'll handle them if they show, though."

"Fine by me," Nance said. "The less contact I have with these alien microbe-ridden people, the happier I am."

"I take it that you're not going onstation, then?" Finaeus asked.

"Not if I can help it," Nance replied. "And I know why you don't want me meeting the team, Jessica. It's so I don't spook them; but if you think you'll get me on that station without this thing on"—with that Nance patted her helmet—"then you're off your fucking rocker."

"Uh…OK," Cargo said as Nance turned and walked off the bridge.

"Strong reaction," Cheeky muttered.

"You can say that again," Finaeus replied.

"Strong—" Cheeky began but stopped abruptly when her statement was met with more than one "Don't!"

"You guys are no fun," Cheeky said with a mock pout. "And here I am still recovering from my ordeal. You should be nicer to me."

INSPECTION

STELLAR DATE: 09.02.8938 (Adjusted Years)
LOCATION: *Sabrina*, Approaching Hermes Station
REGION: Naga System, Orion Freedom Alliance Space

Jessica met the Hermes Station inspection team at the main cargo bay's airlock. As the lock cycled, she examined the team standing within.

There were three women and one man, and Jessica wondered if the prevalence of women over men was present here in Orion space as well, or if this ratio was just a coincidence.

All four wore hazsuits—none as nice as Nance's top-of-the-line models, but still sufficient to deal with serious chemical and biological contaminants.

Per Nance's requirements, Sabrina forced a biohazard sanitization cycle in the lock, and Jessica noticed one of the women shake her head, while another appeared to laugh inside her helmet.

At least they appeared to appreciate the incongruity of the situation.

Jessica really didn't think any of it was necessary. The forty-second century nanotech that protected everyone aboard *Sabrina* was more than up to the task of fighting any contaminants that these four could bring in. Nevertheless, dealing with sanitization in the airlock was easier (and much more pleasant) than listening to Nance complain about all the possible things that could end up growing inside the walls.

As the lock finished its cycle and the main bay doors slid aside, Jessica glanced at her outfit to make certain it was clean and presentable.

She wore the purple shipsuit she had lifted off the Transcend soldier back on Gisha station. Iris had since upgraded it to protect against vacuum and added a ballistic absorption layer, all while keeping the thickness under half a millimeter.

Additionally, all of the logos and tech linking the clothing to the Transcend had been removed, along with the illuminated triangle over the ass. Jessica had no problem with people staring at her rear end, but it didn't need an arrow pointing it out.

A last-minute addition was an emblazoned blue tulip on the collar, something Cheeky had suggested to match their new ship name of the *Matron Tulip*. Not that they really needed a logo—but Cheeky liked to needle Sabrina. A sure sign that the pilot was starting to feel like her old self.

"Welcome aboard," Jessica said as the inspection team stepped into the ship's main bay. "I'm the ship's First Mate, Jessica."

One of the women approached and offered her hand. The inspection team's helmets bore clear faceplates, and Jessica could see a warm, but somewhat wary smile on the woman's face.

<*Hand-shakers too! I've changed my estimate. These people will be wiped out inside of a decade,*> Nance commented privately over the shipnet, apparently observing over the monitoring systems.

<*Hush!*> Jessica admonished.

Jessica accepted the woman's hand and gave it a single, firm shake.

The woman introduced herself and her team, gesturing to each in turn. "Hello, Jessica. I'm Inspector Mary, this is Pete, Lana, and Rory."

"Nice to meet you folks," Jessica said. "The Dockmaster's office said that you want to examine our antimatter containment systems?"

Inspector Mary nodded. "Yes, we'll also do some random scans of your cargo and ship, though we're glad to see that you take biocontaminants seriously."

<*Score one for Nance's paranoia,*> Cheeky said with a laugh over the shipnet.

"Of course," Jessica nodded. "I'll show you to the engine room."

<*You can meet us there, if you want, Nance,*> Jessica said. <*In fact, now that I think about it, it may be weird if you don't.*>

<*Fine, I suppose it'll be safe since these people are suited up—but I'm not shaking hands.*>

Jessica led the Hermes inspection team through the main bay, which was filled with crates—all carefully scrubbed of any Inner Stars origin markers.

The mad dash to make their cargo presentable had been far more hectic than their normal endeavors. Masking the origin of cargo within the Inner Stars was relatively simple—especially since shipping crates seemed to range hundreds of light years from their origin worlds, and it wasn't uncommon to see cargo from one world in crates bearing labels from half a dozen others.

But out here there would be no Inner Stars crates or cargo, and they had only rudimentary information about nearby systems. The crew had decided that, rather than screw up some nuance, the best bet would be to leave off all markings.

It looked extremely suspicious—which the inspection team's curious glances confirmed—but there wasn't much they could do about it now.

"I saw that your ship has been to Naga in the past," Mary said as they walked down the corridor amidships toward the ladder that would take them down to engineering.

"Yeah, we noticed that too," Jessica said, her tone neutral and conversational. "We picked up the *Tulip* just a few years ago—we're still working out some good trade routes and saw this system on the logs. You're a long way out, but sometimes that's where the best opportunities lie."

Mary nodded. "We're always looking for new ships to make runs out here. What do you have onboard?"

The contents of the cargo was something they had spent no small effort sanitizing. Tech was risky because both software and hardware was filled with information belying its origins—even with the most generic of components—and so most of it was floating in the void half a light year back.

Food was less risky, provided certain isotopes were extracted. The end result was a cargo that consisted mostly of melons, dried foodstuffs from various worlds, and some rare gems and minerals—though anyone looking too closely at those would realize that their radiological signatures were from the Orion Arm, not the Perseus Arm of the galaxy.

"Oh, you know, a bit of this and that. Stuff that we hope your folks will like, at least enough for us to buy some good return cargo," Jessica replied.

One of the inspection team members laughed—Lana, if Jessica had interpreted Mary's rapid-fire intros correctly. "We have slime, do you need any slime?"

"Never know," Jessica grinned. "Some people want slime. There's a buyer for almost anything."

"I would imagine that they'll be far more interested in credit—ship like this," Pete said.

"We'd never argue with hard credit, either," Jessica said. "But there's not much profit in hauling credit from one system to another. Never know what might look good to our buyers."

They reached the ladder, and Jessica slid down the rails first, before turning to watch the inspection team descend more carefully, passing their scanning equipment down to Mary who had followed Jessica down.

Jessica couldn't help but notice how both Lana and Pete were taking long looks at her. She had wondered how much she would stand out. Cargo had proposed that he meet with the inspection team, but the crew agreed that Jessica was better at smooth-talking visitors like this.

That had surprised her. Jessica had seen Cargo work a mark more than once, and he was good. That the crew thought she was better was no small compliment.

<*Well, you're a lot more distracting than Cargo is,*> Iris commented, apparently following the gist of Jessica's thoughts.

<*If we were going for distraction, then we should have sent Cheeky down to meet them,*> Jessica replied.

<*Cheeky gets too flustered in situations like this. You remember what happened with that station team that came aboard back on Aldebaran, right?*>

Jessica remembered it well. Aldebaran had been their second stop on the quest to find Finaeus, and had been one near-disaster after another.

For some reason, Cheeky had misread the station's lane designations and came down the wrong approach. They had corrected quickly enough, but the port authority had sent a team to examine their nav systems—claiming they'd flag Cheeky's record if they weren't allowed on the bridge.

Cargo had acquiesced, and when they arrived, Cheeky had been so flustered about her mistake that she lost control of her enhanced pheromone mods. The inspection quickly devolved into the station's team pawing all over Cheeky—as well as Cargo, who had been on the bridge at the time.

It took Sabrina rapid-cycling the air on the ship and switching over to backup filters to get the situation under control. One of the inspectors had threatened to file charges of manipulation, but the others calmed him down. In the end, they had all gone out for drinks.

Even Cargo had gotten lucky that night.

Back in the present, the Hermes Station inspection team had finally reached the base of the ladder and Jessica led them through the doorway into the engineering compartment. Inside, Nance waited with her hazsuit's clear helmet firmly attached and a stoic expression on her face.

"Folks, this is Nance, our engineer and bio. Nance, this is Inspector Mary and her team, Pete, Lana, and Rory," Jessica said, hoping that she had properly identified Lana and Rory.

No one contested her name assignments, and Mary nodded amicably.

"Nice to meet you, Nance," Mary said. "We'll need to look at your antimatter containment, and I'd like to see your flow regulators as well. We like to make sure that you're able to fully shut down your reactor and do a clean startup."

"Of course," Nance said. "Reactor is already offline—we shut it down when we were ten-thousand klicks out, per your regulations."

"We saw that," Mary replied amiably. "Not everyone is so respectful."

Jessica leaned against a bulkhead while Nance showed the inspectors the ship's antimatter bottle, and allowed them to examine the flow regulators.

Lana placed a tamper lock on the bottle, and when they completed their review, Mary gave Nance a quizzical look. "Jessica said you were both engineer and bio, was that correct?"

"It is," Nance nodded. "We run a full hydroponics system on this ship. Plentiful baths and showers on long trips make for great incentives when you want good crewmembers."

"That's unusual," Rory said. "To have full hydroponics on a ship like this, that is."

Nance nodded. "Yeah, but it's one of the things that made a job here appealing for me. I like to manage the tanks as much as the engines."

Mary glanced to Jessica. "Mind if we examine your bio-systems too? It's not strictly necessary, but Nance here seems like a conscientious sort, and if they pass muster, we can lighten the biocontaminant restrictions."

<*We'd better,*> Cargo said over the shipnet. <*They'll get pretty damn suspicious if we try to hide something when showing it would be beneficial to any honest trading ship.* >

<*Fine, but I'm not lowering* **my** *biocontainment restrictions,*> Nance replied.

<*Wouldn't dream of asking it,*> Cargo said.

Nance led the inspectors out of the engine compartment and down the corridor to the environmental systems bay.

Even though Jessica had been aboard *Sabrina* for a decade, she had only been in the environmental bay a few times. Nance guarded it with the fierceness of a mother bear and Jessica had no desire to get on the bio's bad side.

"Wow, this is extensive," Pete said as they walked amongst the tanks, filtration systems, and oxygenation mats.

"How big is your crew again?" Mary asked.

"Six right now," Jessica replied. "We can handle a lot more, though, just haven't found the right folks yet."

"I'll say you can handle a lot more. You could have a hundred people aboard and they'd still get to draw a full bath each day with this setup," Lana said.

"Ship used to be a yacht," Nance supplied. "That's what the previous owners told us, at least."

"Doesn't look much like one," Pete said.

<*Heeeey!*> Sabrina said to the shipnet. <*Jessica, tell them to apologize!*>

<*Why?*> Jessica asked. <*You've always said you hated being a pleasure yacht. That cargo ships have more fun.*>

<*Yeah…but it still wasn't nice.*>

Jessica didn't furnish Sabrina with a reply. Instead she watched as Pete leaned over one of the tanks.

"Lot of these are low. You're missing a lot of biomass," he observed.

"Yeah," Nance said while casting Jessica a worried glance. "I had a bad pump with a bum sensor. It tripped up the flow monitoring systems and I didn't realize we had a problem till there was a full red-algae bloom underway. Last time I buy a pump at Ra—Herschel."

Pete laughed. "Yeah, don't buy shit at Herschel. Those farmers have never met a tolerance requirement that they didn't blatantly ignore."

<*Close one,*> Jessica said. <*Nice save though.*>

<*Thanks, gotta make sure to adjust all my bullshit lines out here. So used to blaming Rattlescar for everything that breaks.*>

<*Looks like Herschel is your new Rattlescar.*>

<*Seems like it,*> Nance replied.

"You know," Mary said, her tone pensive. "One of our local companies may be able to help you with this, with what we have going on down on Marsalla."

"On Marsalla?" Nance asked.

Mary shot her a skeptical look. "Yeah, the photosynthesis plant energy research going on down there."

<*Ohhhh…so that's what they're doing,*> Finaeus said. <*Now I get why they didn't wipe out all the retinol-dependent life.*>

"Oh, the retinol work you're doing, of course," Nance said borrowing from Finaeus's comment and recovering quickly. "I'll admit that it's interesting, but I didn't think it was ready for commercial application."

<*Nice save,*> Cheeky said.

"It's been tricky—from what I hear," Mary began, "but they've finally worked up stable microbes that utilize both chlorophyll and retinol simultaneously to generate energy. They can operate with lower levels of oxygen, and adapt better to different stellar spectra. It could make terraforming worlds under red and blue stars take a lot less bio-tweaking."

<And make for runaway greenhouses,> Finaeus said. *<Been there, done that—though I am interested in their approach. We never tried it with non-terrestrial life in the mix before.>*

<What happened to all your doomsaying about the end of human life at the hands of alien bacteria?> Cheeky asked.

<I'm a scientist. I'm eternally curious,> Finaeus said with a mental shrug. *<You never know, they may have hit on something too.>*

<Out here, at the asscrack of the universe?> Nance asked. *<Seems doubtful.>*

<You'd be surprised what you'll find out on the fringes,> Finaeus replied.

"That does sound rather interesting," Nance said aloud, replying to Mary's statement. "I'll look into it. I will need to pick up more biomass either way. I'll certainly want to give it a look."

"Place looks tip-top," Lana announced from the far end of the compartment. "If our station's environmental systems were this clean I'd take showers over sonic cleans a lot more often."

"Great," Mary said. "We'll just need to look over any organic cargo you have, and we'll be out of your hair."

Jessica saw both Pete and Lana glance over at her purple hair and resisted the urge to sigh. She couldn't be the first person they had ever seen with purple hair.

<Or purple skin, or purple clothes,> Iris commented privately.

<Hey, when you find something you like, embrace it,> Jessica replied. *<Besides, my skin is lavender.>*

<Yes, because that makes it so much better,> Iris laughed.

Jessica led the inspection team back up the ladder into the port-side passageway. She stopped in front of Port-Side Hold #2. Normally they transported produce in stasis—a capability they never advertised in the Inner Stars—what with stasis being lost technology there.

Finaeus had assured them, however, that stasis would be in common usage in Orion space.

Jessica certainly hoped that would be the case as she switched off the stasis field and gestured for the inspection team to enter.

While her team entered the hold, Mary remained in the corridor with Jessica. "Takes a lot of power to run stasis that long. I can see why you have that extra reactor."

<*Not to mention our weapons systems,*> Iris chuckled.

<*Which they better not have spotted,*> Jessica replied. <*Hard to pass ourselves off as a freighter if they spot our railguns.*>

<*We docked at some of the most paranoid stations in the Inner Stars with those things and they never spotted them. The* Intrepid's *engineers did a good job hiding them.*>

"There are some long runs out here," Jessica said. "If we can deliver exotic produce that's still perfectly fresh, we can charge top dollar."

"Watermelon!" Rory called out, speaking for the first time since coming aboard. "I haven't had watermelon in *decades*!"

"If you're interested, we could sell you some of this at cost," Jessica offered.

Mary shot her an appraising look. "Cost?"

Jessica quickly addressed the crew. <*OK folks, is she honest and wants to make sure we're not trying to bribe, or is she dishonest and expects cost to be zero?*>

<*It's a small station. Not everyone can be on the take—or we'd have seen more evidence of that in our chats with the Dockmaster and the tug operator. You made your offer aloud, so her team heard it. If even one of them is honest, then she has to operate above board. So I vote for honesty,*> Cheeky said.

<*I'm with Cheeky,*> Cargo said. <*Plus, I get the honest vibe off her. She hasn't made any of the comments that precede a bribe request.*>

The rest of the crew agreed, and Jessica did some quick calculations in her head. "Well, we got them on a pretty good deal, but you're right about stasis being pricy to run, so, by weight they'll be forty of your local credits per kilo—if my math is right."

"Forty!" Rory called out and Jessica wondered if she had gone too high. "What a steal!"

"A bit low, but it seems reasonable," Mary said with a smile. "Glad to see you weren't trying to offer a bribe, Jessica."

"Glad to see you weren't asking for one," Jessica replied.

Mary laughed and waved to her team. "Rory, they'll set aside a crate. Come pick it up after your shift."

"You guys better," Rory said with a stern look. "I'll be back in three hours with the credit for twenty kilos worth."

<*Stars, what is she doing, running a 'stil?*> Nance asked.

AN AFTERNOON STROLL

STELLAR DATE: 09.02.8938 (Adjusted Years)
LOCATION: Hermes Station
REGION: Naga System, Orion Freedom Alliance Space

Jessica stepped through the airlock and took in the sight of the docking ring's wide sweep. Despite being on the far side of human space, it really didn't look that different from most of the stations she'd seen back in Sol, or in the Inner Stars.

Fewer hawkers were present than on most Inner Stars stations, but there wasn't much foot traffic nearby, and no other ships were docked in any adjacent berths. The station certainly was cleaner than many she had visited in the past, though that was most likely due to the low number of ships that passed through.

Signage pointed to the closest maglev and Jessica reached back for Trevor's hand, grasping it tightly as they walked toward the platform.

"So, if Cargo is finding buyers for all our stuff, what are we doing out here?" Trevor asked.

"What?" Jessica asked, bumping her hip against his thigh. "Getting off the ship isn't reason enough to go for a stroll?"

Trevor chuckled. "I'd stroll anywhere with you Jess, but I know you. You have mission-face."

Jessica shot a wounded look at Trevor. "I do not have mission-face. This is my fun-afternoon-out-on-station face."

"Sure thing," Trevor said and kissed the top of her head.

"Not mollifying me that easily."

"You still haven't said what we're doing out here."

Jessica shrugged. "Just getting the lay of the land, customs, behavior, see if there's anything interesting to buy."

"Like guns?" Trevor chuckled.

"Well, I don't have to buy clothes anymore, you keep me buried in new outfits."

"What can I say?" Trevor shrugged. "I have a gift for fashion—though mostly on you."

Jessica glanced at Trevor, who wore a pair of tight grey pants, a blue shirt—which she knew he'd selected to compliment her coloring—and a long dark coat that tapered back into a tail that ended just above his ankles. The jacket was fitted and made his torso look like a massive triangle, which it largely was, given the width of his shoulders.

"Don't know about that," she replied. "You look pretty delicious yourself."

<OK, you two. I thought organics were supposed to be past this lovey-dovey stage this far into a relationship.>

"Are you kidding?" Trevor chuckled. "I'll never be past that stage with my girl."

"Such a big sap," Jessica said with a smile that contained no displeasure.

"The sappiest," Trevor replied.

"Still," Jessica replied as they walked past a vendor selling a rather curious assortment of meats and pastries. "Keep an eye peeled for hot outfits and mean-looking guns."

"When haven't I?" Trevor replied. "But if you think we're walking past that stall without giving the local cuisine a try, I'll toss you over my shoulder and go over there anyway."

"I'd like to see you try," Jessica chuckled as she turned back toward the vendor002E

"We've fought before. I had to carry you out of the ring."

"I let you beat me. Not to mention the fact that I beat the crap out of just a few people before that fight," Jessica said, her tone indignant.

"Well, I'm not going to fight you again, so we'll have to let that one-time stand," Trevor replied.

"So long as you don't think you can beat me," Jessica muttered as they reached the vendor.

"Welcome to Hermes!" the proprietor, a shorter man with mousy brown hair, said. "I saw you guys come off that new ship! Don't see a lot of new ships around here. Where you from?"

"All over," Jessica replied. "Last stop was Njuen."

"Ah, they have good fish there! Did you bring any fish?"

Jessica shook her head. "I wish we had. We thought you guys were terraforming here. With all that ocean on Marsalla we figured you wouldn't want any fish."

The man chuckled. "Man…if we did have fish down there, I sure wouldn't eat them. A bit too much experimentin' going on down there for my liking."

"The whole retinol-chlorophyll thing, eh?" Trevor asked.

"Yeah, plus other stuff, though you might know that. RHY Dynamics owns the whole world down there. Alotta rumors swirlin' about what they're up to. Sucks too. Most of us moved out here because we thought they were terraforming—you know, for the chance to get some dirt planetside. But that place is off limits…not that any of us would want to go down there, anyway."

"Well, yeah," Jessica said. "From what I hear, playing at mixing alien and terrestrial life is pretty risky stuff."

"Yeah, no shit," the man replied. "Try telling that to RHY, though. Those guys don't give a shit, and they have people up high in the government too. We've sent a lot of petitions to the OFA—even up to the Praetor's office—but nothing ever comes back. I guess they don't care much about us out here."

"No love for the little guy," Jessica nodded.

"So where does the meat come from?" Trevor asked as he eyed one of the meat-filled pastries.

"There are some farms on the moon, all underground. Not great, but it's real livestock, not vat-grown, so there's that."

"I'll try that one," Trevor said. "Anything for you Jessica?"

"Yeah, but I'll pass on the meat. Just one of those pastries with the yellow stuff…lemon of some sort?"

"Yup, lemon. That we grow on station here."

"Awesome," Jessica replied.

The man placed the food on small paper plates. "That'll be nine-fifty. Make sure you put the plates in the right receptacles. Station is really picky about recycling."

Jessica passed the vendor her token over the Link and authorized the transaction, glad to see that the local bank accounts Cargo had set up using credit drawn against the sale of their produce worked properly.

"Thanks," Trevor said as he picked up his pastry and took a bite. "Mmmmmm, this is great."

"Thanks," the man said. "Stop by any time."

"You can count on it," Trevor said.

Jessica led Trevor back out onto the sweep's foot-traffic boulevard and took a bite of her pastry.

"OK, that is good. That guy can cook."

"Or knows where to buy stuff cheap that he can mark up," Trevor replied.

"Or that," Jessica nodded. "Either way, a nice change."

"For sure, been a while since I've had meat that was on the hoof at some point."

As they walked, Jessica drew a few long looks from the locals, the attention nearly making her feel self-conscious. It wasn't as though mods were uncommon. Besides the usual rainbows of skin and hair colors, she saw a man with comically large horns, and two women with tails. She did notice a dearth of people with her coloring—perhaps it had to do with the retinol experimentation on the planet's surface, and people's distrust of the RHY Dynamics company doing it.

They reached the maglev platform in short order, and boarded a car headed to Hermes Station's central spire. Jessica took a seat and leaned back, before letting out a long groan.

Before her, on the forward wall of the maglev car was holo-ad for 'Retyna, a Division of RHY Dynamics'. Front and center, twirling about in the ad, was a woman with purple skin, purple hair, and a purple outfit not that dissimilar to Jessica's own shipsuit.

"Oh, for fucksakes," Jessica muttered.

Trevor's eyes followed her gaze and when they alighted on the ad he burst into laughter.

"OK, OK, it explains a few things," Jessica said.

Trevor didn't reply, his laughter intensifying, tears beginning to stream down his face.

"Really?" Jessica asked, beginning to flush as people on the car turned to stare.

"If…if you…if," Trevor gasped between bursts of laughter. He sucked in a deep breath, trying to regain his composure. "If you ever need a side giiiig!"

The laughter resumed, and several other people on the car began to chuckle.

Jessica sighed. "Yeah, just what I need, my face plastered all over every holodisplay in Orion Space."

<It would give us a legitimate stream of income,> Iris said. *<If Cargo has trouble trading, that is.>*

<Not you too.>

After she drove an elbow into Trevor's ribs he managed to get his laughter under control, and they rode in silence—aside from periodic chuckles from Trevor—until the car stopped at a station in the central spire.

Jessica and Trevor spent the next few hours walking through the station's main commerce district, sampling more food, stopping in a bar for drinks, spending some time in clothing stores, and noting subtle aspects of the local culture.

"One thing's for sure," Trevor said as he took a bite of another meat pastry they picked up at a small bakery. "These folks are omnivores. Vegans would not fare well here."

"I've noticed that too," Jessica said. "I wonder if it's a fringe thing. A desire for a more agrarian society—even if some big corporation is using the planet below for a lab."

"Could be," Trevor noted, then pointed down the wide corridor at a storefront ahead. "Hey, check that place out."

Jessica looked where Trevor was pointing and saw a store with its holodisplay advertising natural leather products.

"Huh, must be from all the food 'on the hoof' as that first guy mentioned. Might as well do something with the skins."

"I bet you'd look great in that jacket," Trevor said, pointing to a black jacket with an angled zipper and a belt at the bottom. "Let's go try it out."

Jessica sighed and followed Trevor, though her reticence was mostly for show. The jacket did look nice—if a bit retro.

They walked into the store, and Jessica took a deep breath, savoring the scent of fresh leather. It was strong, but it had a very 'real' quality to it. Something not easily faked.

Trevor threaded his way through the racks to the jackets in the back, and pulled one off its hanger, holding it out to Jessica.

"Not sure this is going to work," Jessica said as she turned and slipped her arms into the sleeves. "My ratio's a bit off for most off-the-rack clothing."

"Don't I know it," Trevor chuckled. "You're a nightmare to shop for."

Jessica did up the zip—or tried to. The waist was baggy; the natural leather had no stretch, and no hope of closing over her breasts.

Trevor stroked his chin. "Yeah, that's not going to work. If I go a size down it's going to look like a bolero on you."

"Bummer, though," Jessica said as she stroked the sleeve. "It feels really nice."

"Can I help you?" a man said as he approached.

"No—" Jessica began, but Trevor interrupted her.

"Maybe," Trevor said. "Do you do any custom work?"

"Of course!" The man said as he eyed Jessica's waist and amble breasts. "And I can see a custom fit is required. There's a three-hundred credit charge. We do all alterations by hand."

<*Three hundred!*> Jessica exclaimed privately to Trevor. <*I could fab my own jacket for ten credits worth of raw material!*>

<*Yeah, but where's the fun in that?*> Trevor asked. "Deal," he said to the man.

"Excellent," the man said as he looked Jessica up and down. "If you'd hold out your arms and turn please?"

Jessica sighed and complied as the man scanned her, taking the measurements with his eyes—an amusing incongruity for a store that hand-made their clothing.

Trevor concluded the transaction, and the man assured them that he would have the jacket delivered to their ship the next day.

As they left the store, Jessica stifled a yawn. <*Speaking of the ship, I think I'm just about ready to head back. Later tonight I want to hit that bar we passed on the docking ring—gonna need a nap before that. Gonna need to turn on some charm to get the other merchants to spill their best trade routes.*>

<*And get a regional dark-layer map,*> Trevor said. <*The station just had a local update on their dark matter and jump point positions; but that doesn't give us more than a path to the next star.*>

<*Yeah, it'll take—*>

"Excuse me, miss. Hello!" a high-pitched voice called out from behind them.

They turned to see a man and a woman rushing down the corridor smiling and waving.

"Yes?" Jessica asked with an arched eyebrow.

"Hi, thanks for stopping," the woman said as the pair neared. "We couldn't help but notice…well…you!"

"Me?" Jessica asked.

"Yes, yes, you look fantastic, you're absolutely perfect," the man said.

"Thanks," Jessica grinned. "I like to think so, glad you agree."

Trevor stifled a laugh. "Any reason why you stopped to tell us that?"

"Oh yes, of course, this must seem strange," the woman said. "We represent Retyna, you've heard of us, yes?"

"First day on station, but it's been hard not to have spotted your ads," Jessica said.

The man chuckled. "Yes, I suppose you'd notice those."

"That's why we stopped you," the woman said. "We're here working on our plans for when Retyna hits the open market. Interviews with the scientist, sens-recordings of the facilities and the like. But our current Retyna Girl is just a sim. These terraforming types appreciate authenticity…the real deal."

"So what? You want me to model for you?" Jessica asked with a laugh.

"Yeah!" the man said brightly. "You must get a lot of offers. You look amazing."

Jessica did get a lot of offers, but usually not for modeling. Most of the stations they frequented were not populated by people looking for that sort of talent.

"She does, doesn't she," Trevor said with a smile as he glanced at Jessica. "You should do it, Jess, it would be a blast."

<*Stop it!*> Jessica admonished.

<*Would be a good way to blend in, you'd be the public face of a company.*> Iris said.

<*Are you kidding?*> Jessica asked. <*That's the exact opposite of a good way to blend in.*>

<Ever heard of hiding in plain sight?> Trevor asked.

"Thanks for the offer," Jessica said. "But I don't think it will work out. We won't be on Hermes for long,"

"We could schedule it soon, how does tomorrow sound?"

"Yes!" Trevor replied.

"No! He's kidding. We have to go, c'mon, Trevor."

Trevor laughed as Jessica pulled him away, calling back to the confused-looking Retyna employees. "Sorry, I tried!"

* * * * *

"This is officially my least favorite station of all time," Jessica said as she collapsed into a chair in *Sabrina*'s galley.

Nance and Cheeky were present, both picking at the left-overs from a meal that had been prepared and consumed while Jessica and Trevor were out.

"Why's that?" Nance asked.

"I bet I know," Cheeky said, snorting a laugh.

<Aww, it's her snort-laugh,> Sabrina said. *<This must be good.>*

"You have no idea," Cheeky giggled. "Jessica is a shoe-in for a job at this local company called Retyna."

"I repeat. Why's that?" Nance said.

Cheeky flicked her wrist and a Retyna ad appeared over the table, eliciting another giggle from Cheeky and a laugh from Nance.

"Wow, Jessica, if you ever needed another job…"

"Oh, you have no idea," Jessica said with a sigh. "They actually approached me for one. I guess with their whole schtick being retinol's purpleness and all that, their corporate image is this purple girl. In their ads they say she powers her internal mods with retinol photosensitive skin."

"What? So, they want you to turn your skin into some sort of retinol plant-based thing?" Nance asked, her face a mixture of horror and curiosity.

"I have no idea!" Jessica said. "I got the hell away as fast as I could. I don't think I'm going back on station while we're here."

"Could always just change your skin and hair to another color," Cheeky said. "With your nanotech it wouldn't take long."

Jessica nodded as she held up her hand and turned it over. "Yeah, it wouldn't be hard. But this is something that reminds me of Trist and our time on Victoria. I know I have Trevor now…and I love him a lot, but Trist and…we spent almost seventy years together."

"That's a long time," Cheeky said with a nod. "You were with her longer than I've been alive."

"Yeah, I just like it as a memory of her…and now it reminds me of new memories with Trevor too. I know it's silly—"

"It's not," Nance said, interrupting Jessica. "None of us have a lot to tie ourselves to in this 'verse. We're like leaves on the wind. Stuff like that? Those special memories. They're important and it's OK to hold onto them."

"What she said," Cheeky added.

"Thanks, Nance, Cheeks," Jessica said with a smile. "You two are the best."

"Yeah, I know," Cheeky said.

"There you all are," Cargo said as he walked into the galley. "We're in a right mess here."

"Oh yeah?" Jessica asked. "Worse than the usual?"

Cargo grunted sourly as he sat. "Maybe. Seems you can't just scoop fuel in this system. You have to pay a fee to some company that has a lock on that business. Since we can't sell half our cargo, and we have to buy stuff to maintain our fiction as a trader, we don't have the credit to scoop. Not at the rates I just got quoted."

"Could just scoop off the star when we pass by anyway," Cheeky said. "What are they gonna do, chase us down?"

"Doesn't really help us stay under the radar," Jessica replied. "What sort of company has a monopoly on scooping anyway? Whatever people don't scoop just gets washed away in the stellar wind. It's not like you can use it all without building a dyson sphere."

"I don't know," Cargo said as he rubbed his thumbs against his temples. "Some company called RHY Dynamics. The rate they charge is crazy too, it's as much as we'll make from selling all our cargo."

"Awwwww shit," Jessica muttered.

<Jessica? There's a call for you from the company you were talking about.>

"Which one? RHY or Retyna?" Jessica asked, knowing it didn't really matter.

<Retyna.>

Jessica groaned. "Kay, put it on the table, but just show me. No need to let them know they have an audience to play off."

A moment later the image of the woman who had approached Jessica in the corridor outside the leather shop appeared above the table.

"Jessica! Hello, I'm so glad I found you. It took a bit of digging, but Mary at the inspection office got me your name and your ship."

<Couldn't have been that hard,> Iris said. *<I bet a hundred people could have told her where to find you.>*

"Hi…you have me at a disadvantage…" Jessica said.

"Oh! Of course. We didn't have a chance to get properly introduced before. I'm Phoebe, I run the marketing group at Retyna—though you might have guessed that," Phoebe's voice rose up at the end of her statement, squeaking a bit.

"I wouldn't have guessed that you *ran* it," Jessica said with a sigh.

"Yeah! My uncle owns RHY and put me in charge of marketing Retyna's new products. Like I'd mentioned, we're just through our final trials, so I'm out here to get interviews from the scientists, images down on the planet, that sort of thing. Running into you on Hermes was pure serendipity."

<*Someone shoot me,*> Jessica said over the shipnet.

"I thought I told you that I really wasn't interested in being your spokesmodel," Jessica said.

Phoebe gave an endearing smile. "Yeah, but I just figured you were playing hard to get. Thing is, we've been building up this whole Retyna Girl persona and how she has our patented Retyna in her skin that she uses to supercharge herself! It's really cool, except putting Retyna right in someone's skin isn't something we can recommend…yet, There might be side effects."

"I can imagine," Jessica replied.

"Right! Of course, you can. Thing is, like I mentioned these terraforming buyers we're targeting are very salt-of-the-earth types. They like real things, not sims, so we wanted to get a real model."

"I imagine that you can afford to get all sorts of models for this, though," Jessica said. "What's so appealing about me?"

"Well…you, of course! You may have noticed that with retinol making plants purple, making purple appealing is our thing—hence Retyna Girl. And trust me, Jessica, you *are* the very definition of appealing."

"I'm still not interested," Jessica said.

<*Wait a second,*> Cargo interjected privately. <*You realize what this squeaky little bitch is doing, right? They're extorting us—and they have us over a barrel. You have to do this. What's the big deal, it's just some posing, reciting some lines, letting them use your image for ads and stuff.*>

<*Well, for starters, it totally blows any incognito cover I have,*> Jessica said.

<*We're going to be racing across Orion space as fast as possible. We'll be out of their sphere of influence in no time,*> Cargo said. <*Jessica, you have to do this. We'll trade your modeling for a free scoop off the star and we'll be free and clear, and on our way.*>

<*Stars, Cargo, you owe me. **Everyone** owes me.*>

While she had been debating with Cargo, Phoebe had continued extolling the virtues of Retyna and how amazing it would be for Jessica to become Retyna Girl; that it would be more exciting than anything she had ever done before.

However, before Jessica could state that she would do the job, Phoebe's voice lowered, becoming decidedly less squeaky.

"You may have noticed how it's rather expensive to get fuel in this system," she said. "I can take care of that for you, you know…or make it worse."

"How much better?" Jessica asked. "The kind of better I'm thinking of is the free kind."

Phoebe's pixie-like features pinched as she frowned. "You drive a hard bargain, Jessica, but I'll see that it's done. I'm leaving Hermes tomorrow night, so we'll want to do the shoot tomorrow and the surgery tonight."

"Whoa!" Jessica cried out. "You never said anything about surgery!"

"Well yeah, silly. You have to become Retyna Girl, with our patented Retnya *in* your skin. It's part of why you're so perfect—the total package! You don't have organic skin, so we can embed our product in it without any risks. It'll actually work too. It pulls a lot of energy out of light, it may make your skin a bit lighter, but you can adjust how active it is too. You'll be a powerhouse!"

<*It should be safe enough,*> Nance said. <*I mean, I wouldn't ever let them do it to me, but you're hardly organic to begin with anymore.*>

<Nance! It's an alien organism. You and Finaeus were both very much against this sort of thing—or was I dreaming all that.>

<I've been researching it since Mary was aboard with her team. I think they may be on to something here. Finaeus does too. We'll make sure Iris knows what to look out for. You'll be perfectly safe. Worst case scenario, Iris can use your nano to expunge it,> Nance replied.

<True, I could,> Iris agreed. *<Stop being such a baby and just do it.>*

<Just make sure they take it back out of you before you come back to the ship,> Nance added.

Jessica sighed and met Phoebe's eyes. "Fine. Send the address for where this is all going to happen."

"You got it! I'll see you in an hour!" Phoebe transmitted the location over the Link and then signed off.

"This is the worst idea ever," Jessica sighed.

"Well, we could raise a stink and shoot our way clear across Orion space," Cargo said, sarcasm oozing from his voice. "I don't get why you're not OK with this, Jessica. Seems right up your alley."

"Besides, it's like you're going to be a superhero! Retyna Girl!"

Jessica leveled a long stare at Cheeky. "When this is over, we never speak of it again."

Cheeky reached out and pinched Jessica's cheek. "Whatever you say, Retyna Girl."

UPGRADE

STELLAR DATE: 09.02.8938 (Adjusted Years)
LOCATION: Hermes Station
REGION: Naga System, Orion Freedom Alliance Space

"Jessica! Thanks for making it on time," Phoebe said, extending her hand as Jessica walked through the doors.

"That's me. Punctual," Jessica replied.

The area of the station Phoebe's directions had led her to appeared to be the main RHY offices on the station, a clean—if a little bland—facility near the top of the central spire. It was, thankfully, devoid of any ads featuring Retyna Girl.

"Of course!" Phoebe exclaimed. "Retyna Girl is always punctual!"

"Is that one of her super powers?" Jessica asked dryly.

"Uh…no," Phoebe said.

<*Be nice,*> Iris said.

<*I wish Trevor could be here,*> Jessica replied. <*I'd feel better if backup was closer.*>

<*He's managing cargo transfers while Cheeky and Cargo are at that bar seeing if they can get a dark layer map. Nance still won't leave the ship, and Finaeus can't, so you're on your own. Think you can do it? Got your big girl pants on?*>

<*Shut up, Iris,*> Jessica said sourly, then chuckled. She really was acting like a baby. But something about being forced to perform bothered her. Well, not something. She knew the reason she felt uneasy, but the reason was over a hundred years old now. That undercover op back on High Terra shouldn't be affecting her thinking so much—rather, she shouldn't *let* it affect her so much. <*Iris…sorry, you're right.*>

<*I know I am. Now, pay attention, Phoebe is being all excited telling you about how amazing Retyna Girl is, you need to act like this isn't a death sentence.*>

<*Unless the microbes kill me,*> Jessica said.

<*Jessica!*>

<*OK, OK!*>

"So how does all that sound?" Phoebe asked. "I hope you can do our girl justice. She's strong and powerful, she doesn't take any shit, but she's also nice, kay, we need you to be nice as well as strong."

Jessica relaxed her shoulders and gave Phoebe a winning smile. "I can be nice, I promise. This is going to rock. Retyna Girl is going to be a hit across the whole OFA."

"Oh! That's great! You look so pretty when you smile!" Phoebe gushed as she leaned forward and wrapped Jessica in an embrace. She pulled back and swept her eyes down Jessica's body. "I mean, you look hot all the time, but extra pretty when you smile."

The next half hour was spent with the RHY lawyers, examining the contract, ensuring that it included the waiver of scoop fees for *Sabrina*—rather, the *Matron Tulip*—and even some nice residual royalties for Jessica over the next few years from any derivative works that used her likeness.

<*That's not really necessary,*> Jessica said after her AI proposed the final round of changes.

<*It would be if you were really from around here. Besides, you never know when a bit of extra credit will come in handy.*>

Once the contract was signed, and the station had the waiver of scoop fees on record, Jessica let the ever-bubbly Phoebe lead her down a long series of corridors, past offices to areas filled with labs. Most were occupied by automatons managing cultures, though there were some human workers present as well.

Eventually Phoebe led her into a room where two women in white hazsuits waited before a table.

"Here we are! Jessica…I mean Retyna Girl." Phoebe corrected herself with a giggle. "I'd like you to meet Doctors

Kimbal and Betty. They'll be doing the work to turn you into our hero!"

Betty gave a warm smile, but Kimbal just frowned.

"Let's get to it, we're already behind and I have things to do other than marketing stunts."

"Oh, Kim," Betty said with a smile. "This'll be fun. It's our first human implantation!"

"First?" Jessica asked.

"Oh, well first full coverage. We've done bits before. It's when we realized that someone with an artificial skin would be a better candidate. And you're perfect!"

"Uh, thanks," Jessica replied.

<I've faced down admirals and fleets and all sorts of crap. How come these two doctors scare the shit out of me?>

<Don't worry, I'll keep an eye on everything. I can shut down their whole operation if I have to. We out-tech these people ten to one. Speaking of which, they don't know about me yet, and I think that we'd best keep it that way. In the Inner Stars they couldn't tell that I wasn't just a run-of-the-mill AI, but here they might notice.>

<OK, I'm trusting you…but if I wake up with tentacles, or mushrooms growing out of me, I'm gonna be pissed.>

"Please, lay down so we can get started. It won't take too long," Doctor Kimbal said, gesturing to the table. "Oh, but you'll need to disrobe, of course."

Jessica nodded and pulled off her shipsuit—not the purple one, no point in risking it along with her wellbeing. Once naked, she lay down on the table, and Betty pressed a hypospray against her neck. "Just something to put you under for a bit."

<Wake me if they do anything crazy,> Jessica admonished Iris.

<Don't worry, I'm in here too, you know.>

As consciousness slipped away, Jessica heard Phoebe say, "Oh, and do something about her blue eyes, Retyna Girl has to have purple eyes."

Fuck.

CONFESSIONS

STELLAR DATE: 09.02.8938 (Adjusted Years)
LOCATION: Hermes Station
REGION: Naga System, Orion Freedom Alliance Space

Jessica woke with a start, her arms stretching out, reaching for the edge of the bed. They found it, and confirmed that it was indeed a bed.

She tried to look around, but couldn't see a thing, not even when cycling her vision.

<*Shit, did they blind me?*>

<*No, they put gauze over your eyes after they changed them to purple. Well, they thought they changed them to purple, but I did it instead. I didn't want them to mess up your vision, so when they injected some short-term dye, I made it stick, rather than having your nano scrub it out like it wanted to,*> Iris replied.

<*Can I take the gauze off? Is it safe to look? Did they…damage me?*>

<*Well…you're going to have to see for yourself,*> Iris replied hesitantly.

<*Oh dear…*>

Jessica peeled the gauze from her eyes and waited for them to adjust. It took only a moment before she could make out a darkened room lit by a purple glow.

A purple glow.

Jessica raised her right hand and let out a long sigh.

<*My skin is glowing, Iris. Is that the worst of it, or is there something else I should know?*>

<*Nope, that's actually the only significant side-effect. They didn't expect it, either. From what I can discern it has to do with a reaction to the polymers your skin is made out of. I suspect I can mute it, but I don't want to tip our hand as to the nano you have.*>

<*Thanks, Iris. Does the stuff work?*> Jessica asked as she lifted her leg into the air, wiggling her toes and watching the light dance on the ceiling.

<*Yeah, it's amazing, to be honest. These microbes are really efficient. Your skin is like a high-output solar panel now. I'd say it has ninety-percent conversion efficiency with very low heat transference. You could actually charge your internal batteries off this without too much trouble.*>

<*Think they'll let me keep it?*> Jessica asked. <*Contract said that it had to get removed after the shoot, but this is really cool.*>

<*If it's just the glowy skin that's getting you so excited, you can get that done without having alien microbes embedded in you.*>

<*Well, it's also kinda tingly in a nice way,*> Jessica said as she rubbed her thighs.

<*Easy girl. It's still five hours 'til they said they'd come in to wake you. Why don't you just go to sleep,*> Iris suggested.

<*Yeah, sleep. Like I can do something like that right now.*> Jessica ran a hand down up her side, cupping her right breast. <*Oh…I wonder if this is how Sera's skin makes her feel all the time. No wonder she never changed it back.*>

Iris chuckled. <*And here you were complaining like a whiny child about this whole thing and now it's turning you on.*>

<*Well, I still don't want to be their Retyna Girl tomorrow, but I'll take the skin. Trevor is going to love this.*>

Iris's avatar frowned in Jessica's mind. <*I don't get it. You live to put yourself on display; people call you a sex doll and you laugh. But this offer comes along and you completely freak out—and that was before you even knew about the alien microbes. What gives?*>

<*Wow, you're such a buzzkill,*> Jessica moaned. <*I was just about to get somewhere.*>

<*Stop changing the subject. Spill it.*>

Jessica sighed and closed her eyes. <*It was back when I was in the Terran Bureau of Investigation. I was still pretty raw, but I had some wins under my belt. I got sent on an undercover op to deal with a memory-thief ring—you know the people who steal memories, wipe them from the people who made them, and then sell them off?>*

<*I'd heard of that, yeah,*> Iris replied. <*Seems pretty risky, for both parties.*>

<*Yeah, it was. Mostly for the person who had their memories stolen. The thieves weren't too careful, and they trashed people's brains a lot when they did it…*> Jessica drew a hand to her forehead, starting when her skin tingled in response. <*Gah, that's going to take some getting used to.*>

<*So what happened?*> Iris sounded genuinely curious about the tale.

<*Well, I found out some places where they hung out, and I bought some memories—I don't have them anymore, but I remember feeling vile about the whole thing. We managed to return most of them to their owners, though not everyone had enough mental capacity anymore to reaccept them.*

<*Anyway, I managed to work my way up toward a mid-level guy. He was working his own way up the chain, and I figured I could stick with him to find the people at the top. Their tech was just too good for the putz I'd set up with to be running the show.*

<*Thing is, he liked girls modded. Like modded a lot. He freaked me right up, tentacles, more eyes, crazy shit, and then he made me perform, dance, do full-sensory stuff, humans, bots, crazy modded people. Some really vile…. Anyway, I don't remember most of it anymore because he sold the memories—thank stars. But I remember how I felt, how I still feel when I think of it.*>

Iris wrapped Jessica in a warm mental embrace. <*I'm sorry that happened to you. I can see how getting modded and performing for other people would bother you now.*>

<*Yeah,*> Jessica said. <*I know it's not the same, but it kinda is, right? We're being extorted to do it. When I was in deep, the TBI wouldn't pull me. They wanted me to get to the top. I eventually did and I took that sucker down. I don't remember it because after the*

trials, the TBI stripped those memories. One of my co-workers told me I shoved my tentacles down the throat of the woman who ran the whole thing and tore her insides out.>

<*Holy shit, Jessica!*> Iris exclaimed. <*Though, I guess if you kept your job it must have been warranted in some fashion. Still, having gone through all that, I'm really surprised that you didn't get the TBI to put you back the way you were before all that started.*>

<*Well, do you see extra eyes and tentacles?*> Jessica chuckled softly in her mind. <*Anyway, I had more work scheduled to get back to the way I was, but then another mission came up, and my CO needed me on it, so I went in pretty much as you know me—minus the lavender skin that I picked up back at Victoria.*>

Jessica managed a weak smile, glad that most of those old memories from the TBI were gone, but something she had learned over the years was that pain could outlast memory.

<*That's cold. I can't believe your CO did that to you.*>

<*Yeah, she was a heartless bitch. Passed over for promotion for so long that she just decided that she would ruin everyone beneath her. She lost her job in the end. Killed herself a few years later—dove off High Terra in a star-surfing suit and just augured herself into the Earth.*>

<*Wow, the story just gets better...but why did you keep yourself modded...and if I may be frank, keep fucking everything that moved?*>

Jessica laughed. <*It happened on that next assignment that my CO put me on. She used me because I was sexed up and broken. I was so broken...I really thought that my value existed only in fucking. I mean, it's what had been drilled into my head for a year undercover—and then my boss used me for it too.... I figured that if I was doing crazy shit and banging everything in sight I was doing what I was supposed to. But somehow on that mission I realized what was happening to me—I mean, I always knew, but somehow I managed to rise above it.*

<Here's the thing. I liked sex. A lot. Always have—its why I got that first undercover assignment. But what I figured out is that I didn't have to give control through sex. Instead, I realized that **I** *could take it. Let's just say that the pendulum swung the other way—waaaay the other way.>*

Jessica chuckled at some of the memories, at the crazy things she'd done in the past, what felt like lifetimes ago.

<After that second undercover op, they put me in a lot of therapy, but even so, the TBI still had no issues with leveraging my proclivities. However, after my bitch-boss was fired, I managed to get into a unit that dealt with more serious crimes, which is how I got on the Myrrdan case.

<I won't lie. I was still pretty broken when he dumped me on the Intrepid. *I didn't think so, but I was. Myrrdan probably knew it too. Either way, that was the best thing that ever happened to me. Myrrdan was living trash, the worst thing ever, but what he did saved me.>*

<How?> Iris asked.

<Tanis found me in that stasis tube, and she instantly accepted me. I mean, she may have made a comment here or there about my appearance, but it was more to show that she acknowledged who I was, and that it was OK. She put me to work. With my brain, not my body, working leads, analyzing data. She trusted me and introduced me to Trist….>

Jessica's thoughts wandered for a moment, remembering those early days on the *Intrepid* as it drifted through the darkness between Estrella de la Muerte and The Kap. Tears formed in the corners of her eyes, and she stared at the roof, watching the light on the ceiling sparkle and shift as the salty droplets flowed down her luminescent skin.

<She saved me, Iris. I owe Tanis everything. Now we're out here…. Ten thousand light years from home. A home I've never seen, just one that I hope to see some day…. And here I am getting modded for someone else's pleasure and purpose. And performing for them.>

<*I understand,*> Iris said. <*And you understand too, I can tell. Even though we're being forced into this, you're not doing it for some government agency, for an asshat CO that is using you to punish someone else for her failings. You're doing it for your crewmates. And to get home, to see Tanis and the* Intrepid *again.*>

Jessica nodded. <*I am, you're right. This is just a means to an end. It doesn't change me. I'm an ocean and this is just a storm. When it passes, I will remain as I always have. Implacable and unchanged.*>

<*I like the metaphor,*> Iris said. <*Now, why don't you relax and go back to sleep. Morning will be here soon enough. You'll become Retyna Girl, you'll own it, make it yours; you'll not become theirs. We'll get our fuel, and our map, and we'll get the hell out of this place and back home.*>

Jessica laughed softly. <*I'm going to be kicking some serious ass as Retyna Girl. They're never going to be able to cast anyone for the role again without them looking like a pale shadow.*>

<*That's the spirit,*> Iris replied, sending soothing waves into Jessica's mind as she drifted back to sleep.

A MAN NAMED MISHA

STELLAR DATE: 09.02.8938 (Adjusted Years)
LOCATION: Hermes Station
REGION: Naga System, Orion Freedom Alliance Space

"Looks like our sort of place," Cheeky said as she sauntered toward the bar and selected a stool. "Just enough seediness, but we're not likely to get into a fight."

"Pretty sure our kinda place is a lot seedier than this," Cargo replied as he sat beside her.

Cheeky pulled at the hem of her short skirt as she hooked her heels over the stool's bottom ring. "Maybe for you, but I tend to go a bit upscale. I prefer to hang with people who wash more than the folks *you* circulate amongst."

"Yeah, but my kind of people have the goods we want to trade in to make money," Cargo said as the bartender—a human, not servitor—approached.

"Hey, what'll it be?"

Cheeky eyed the black-haired woman, giving her slender arms and long neck a second glance. Anyone could have a great rack, or nice ass; but getting the arms toned just right, and having a kissable neck were harder to pull off. She appreciated the little things.

"Whisky. Rocks," Cargo said.

"Your best vodka. Top shelf," Cheeky added. "I have some celebrating to do."

"Oh yeah?' the bartender asked as she turned to pull a bottle off the shelf behind her. "Whatcha celebratin'?"

"Being alive," Cheeky replied with a smile. "Had a close brush with death, not too long ago."

"That why you got that plastic skin?" the woman asked as she poured out Cheeky's drink and slid it over to her.

"Yeah, gotta wait for the next regen to get my own stuff back," Cheeky said. The statement wasn't quite true; the *Intrepid*'s rather impressive nanotech was growing her new skin beneath her artificial epidermis. Which itched like all fuck, but she would grin and bear it while working the bar crowd. Nothing less attractive than a grown woman scratching herself like a monkey in heat.

<*I don't think they do that when in heat,*> Piya noted.

<*Stay out of my metaphors,*> Cheeky laughed.

"Sounds harsh," the woman said as she slid Cargo his whisky. "Tab?"

"This should cover it," Cargo said as he placed a two-hundred credit chit on the counter.

"Was wondering when we'd get to that part of the conversation," the woman smiled.

<*She's got a good smile, maybe I should stick around 'til her shift ends. Though I don't know if I'm quite up to a tousle in the sack yet.*>

<*Stay focused,*> Piya said with a smile.

<*I am focused. On the idea of nibbling at her ears.*>

<*I think she's more into Cargo,*> Piya said as the bartender leaned over the counter, her face a dozen centimeters from the captain's.

"I haven't seen many men with skin like yours," she said as she ran a hand through her long hair as it fell over her shoulders and pooled on the surface of the bar. "Is it true what they say?"

<*Well that escalated quickly,*> Cargo said.

<*Roll with it, don't lose the moment!*> Cheeky said, patting Cargo on the shoulder and turning away to look out over the crowd.

<*Oh hey, she just bit my cheek!*> Cargo exclaimed.

<Yeah, I just dosed you with some pheromones when I touched you. If she doesn't climb on your lap in the next minute, I'll eat my dress.>

<Damnit, Cheeky, I was looking forward to this whiskey.>

<Cargo, you haven't been laid in at least a year. It's making you one grumpy SOB. Go fuck her brains out and meet me back on the ship.>

<What about intel, isn't that what we're here for?>

<Well yeah, haven't you ever heard of pillowtalk?> Cheeky shook her head. *<If you're gonna be the captain of the SS* Sexy, *you're going to have to up your game.>*

*<We are **not ever** calling the ship that.>*

Cheeky watched out of the corner of her eye as the woman swung up over the bar and landed on Cargo's lap. She proceeded to press her lips into his as a servitor emerged from a back door to take over.

The woman slid off Cargo and pulled him though another door around the side of the bar, and Cheeky took a sip of her vodka.

It wasn't bad stuff, actually made from potatoes too, just like it should be.

<Sooo…who should I go pay a visit to?> she mused while surveying the tables and their assembled patrons.

"Hey, looks like you got abandoned by your friend there," a voice came from her right.

Cheeky turned to see a slender man settle on the stool vacated by Cargo only moments earlier.

<Dude's like a ninja! I didn't see him at all,> Cheeky exclaimed.

<I did, you were too busy ogling all the other patrons,> Piya replied.

<Not all of them. At least half are not even close to being ogle-worthy.> Then she gave the man next to her a winning smile. "Yeah, looks like he caught someone's attention."

"Clarissa's like that. She's more than happy to give people whatever info they want, but she likes to take her pound of flesh while she's at it."

"A whole pound, eh?" Cheeky asked.

"At least. I'm Misha, by the way," the man said.

He held out his hand, and Cheeky shook it, her grip soft and light, but not limp. "I'm Cheeky."

"Cheeky?" Misha asked. "That's a funny name."

Cheeky wiggled on her stool. "I came by it honestly."

"Oh, I've noticed. I saw you leave your ship a few times. I gotta say, you and your crew are not what I'd expect to see aboard a ship named the *Matron Tulip*."

Cheeky gave a bubbly laugh. "Yeah, we haven't gotten the registry changed yet. But trust me, it's gonna have a much better name. Something that starts with S, I think."

"Dunno," Misha said with a shake of his head. "That one woman—the purple one—seemed to be proudly wearing a tulip emblem."

"Yeah, she lost a bet."

Misha laughed as the servitor handed him a drink and he took a sip. "So, enough of all this small talk. What are you in the market for?"

"Market?" Cheeky asked innocently.

"Mizz Cheeky. I don't run a stand on the dock because I like the view—mostly. I deal in info. Who's moving what, where they're moving it to, how long it takes. Out here a leg up on your competitor is make or break."

"I'll bet," Cheeky said, her lips hidden behind the rim of her glass. "I bet breaking is a lot more common."

Misha shrugged. "Everything tends toward entropy."

"I'll admit, we could use an edge—and better regional dark layer maps. The ones we have around here are way out of date. I'm the pilot aboard the *Tulip*, and if I slam her into some dark matter...well...I guess no one will be upset at me, because they'll be dead."

Misha smiled. "I can see how you'd like to avoid that. I might be able to help."

<Finally! I was starting to wonder if I'd have to drag it out of him. For an info broker, he doesn't seem to know when to take an opening.>

Piya laughed. *<Probably why he's also running a food stand.>*

"So you have DL maps for sale?"

Misha nodded. "And the best shipping routes in the area. Which are a bit sparse, I'll admit, but like I said, if you have an edge...."

Misha took another sip of his drink, and Cheeky wondered about this mousy-haired man. He didn't seem that smooth, and was obviously just a one-person operation. Normally the person selling the intel wasn't the one who gathered it. Made it a bit difficult to gather it the next time.

"So, what's the going rate?" she asked.

"I have a DL map that will show you all the best jump routes for forty parsecs—coreward, of course. There's nothing rimward of here but a few miners scraping some valuable ores off asteroids."

"That may do," Cheeky said, adding a tone of disappointment to her voice. "Gives us some options, at least. How much?"

"Twenty-thousand."

Cheeky was glad that she hadn't taken a sip of her vodka, or she would have spat it out all over the man.

"You've got to be kidding!"

Misha gave Cheeky a knowing smile. "Look, you're not legitimate traders. Everyone knows that. It's why RHY extorted you with those crazy scoop fees, it's why you're selling produce no one anywhere near here grows—which is delicious, I might add. Mary's inspection team couldn't stop talking about how weird your engine compartment looks. If your ship didn't have a legitimate registry you would have been kicked off the station by now."

<OK, so maybe he's a bit better than I gave him credit for,> Cheeky admitted to Piya.

<Seems like that might be the case.>

Even so, Cheeky did not alter her expression of disbelief and stared Misha down.

He gave in first. "OK, OK. I'll tell you what, since I like you guys, and your man is taking his time with Clarissa, I'll give you a deal. Fifteen thousand. *If* you give me a ride to your next stop."

Movement near the door caught Misha's eye and he slipped off the stool toward the back of the bar. "I'll come by your ship tomorrow, thirteen hundred hours station time. I'll have the maps."

Cheeky looked in the mirror behind the bar and saw two tall women walk by the windows outside, and pass through the doorway a moment later.

One of the women was bald with writhing tattoos covering her head, while the other had long white hair that fell down her back in a single, loose braid.

Both were wearing matte black light combat armor, and though they were only carrying pulse pistols—per station law—Cheeky suspected that a few more weapons would be secreted away in their persons.

<We don't want that type of company,> Piya said.

Cheeky couldn't agree more, and rose from her stool, threading the tables in a circuitous route to reach the door without passing the newcomers, but Baldy-Tats spotted her and stepped into her path.

"Where you going, little girl?"

Cheeky saw that Whitey-Braids had taken another route moving around behind her.

"For a stroll on the sweep," Cheeky said. "Getting a bit crowded in here."

"But you didn't finish your drink," Baldy-Tats said, her tattoos changing from black to red as she spoke. "Why don't you come back to the bar and sit with me for a bit?"

Baldy-Tats' tone of voice made it clear that the statement was not a question. Cheeky glanced at the other patrons, and saw that no one so much as looked at the two women, though the volume of conversation had decreased noticeably.

"Umm…sure," Cheeky agreed, giving Baldy-Tats a warm smile. She returned to her seat and grabbed her drink, downing most of it in a single gulp.

The two women sat on either side of her, and Cheeky wondered if the stools would support their large frames and armor. They held, but groaned loudly as the two women settled into place.

Baldy-Tats spoke again. "I'm Mandy, this is Jenn."

Jenn didn't speak, but blew Cheeky a kiss.

"Mind if I call you Baldy-Tats and Whitey-Braid?" Cheeky asked. "It's what I've been thinking to myself as you came in, and I really think they suit you better than Mandy and Jenn."

"Uh, yeah," Baldy-Tats said. "We'd mind a lot."

"Huh, too bad," Cheeky replied.

"Look, we saw that you were talking to a friend of ours," Baldy-Tats continued. "We were hoping to have a chat with him, but imagine our surprise when he ducked out. You wouldn't happen to know where he was off to, would you?"

"Uhhh…maybe headed back to his stand? He runs a food stand down the sweep a ways."

Whitey-Braid smiled and pulled her thick braid over her shoulder, fingers playing with the tuft of hair at the end. "He's our friend, of course we know that."

"What were the two of you talking about?" Badly-tats asked. "Hey, wait, you're from that ship that showed up earlier, aren't you, the *Old Flower*, right?"

"Matron Tulip," Cheeky corrected with a sigh.

"Nothing matronly about you, that's for sure," Whitey-Braid said with a predatory grin.

"So, what were you talking about," Baldy-Tats asked again.

Cheeky chuckled and released a dose of pheromones. "He was trying to convince me that if I let him sample my wares, he'd give me a discount on his and supply us for the first leg of our next trip."

Baldy-Tats barked a laugh, and looked over at Whitey-Braid. "Sounds like Misha. Guy doesn't catch much tail around here."

"Why you so eager to talk to him?" Cheeky asked.

"Oh, we just want to check up on a little business venture," Baldy-Tats said.

"But I think we could put that on hold for a bit and consider another sort of venture," Whitey-Braid said as she reached out and stroked Cheeky's thigh. "I mean…you're the ship's fuck puppet, right? Keep things fun on the long jumps. I think Mandy and I should make sure you're up to the task."

Cheeky laughed. "You'd be surprised what happens on the *Tulip.* Trust me."

Baldy-Tats pressed up behind Cheeky and purred into her ear. "Oh, we don't have to *trust* you, we'd like to find out for ourselves."

<*I think you let loose too many pheromones,*> Piya said.

<*I figured that they were going to beat the shit out of me, this is a much better outcome.*>

<*I wonder if these two have a strongly drawn line between sex and beating the shit out of people,*> Piya mused.

<*Yeah, that would not be a big surprise. Ideas?*> Cheeky asked.

<*Well, try not to leave the bar with them, that's a good start.*>

"Let's go to our ship," Baldy-Tats said as she reached around Cheeky's shoulders to her chest, pinning her right arm.

"Well, you just got me back here to my Vodka, mind if I finish it?"

<Cargo, mayday, I need an assist!>

<You have got to be kidding me!> Cargo retorted. *<You dose me to get this girl to jump my bones—which she's* ***really*** *good at, I might add—and then you want me to stop?>*

<Well, I don't ***want*** *you to stop so much as I don't want to get turned into the meat in a bitch sandwich.>*

"You listening, Tulip Girl?" Baldy-Tats asked as she groped Cheeky's breasts.

"It's Cheeky," she replied.

"She's being more than just a bit cheeky," Whitey-Braid chuckled as she picked up Cheeky's glass and downed the last of the vodka.

"No, Cheeky's my name. I'm Cheeky, not Tulip Girl."

Baldy-Tats guffawed, her armor digging into Cheeky's back. "Oh, that's priceless. You really *are* the sex toy on that ship, aren't you?"

"Well, we were talking about changing its name to the SS *Fuck*." Cheeky smiled.

"Step back, and no, we are not naming the ship that," a voice said from behind the bar.

Cheek's eyes darted to her right, catching the welcome sight of Cargo rising from behind the bar with a handgun held high and near his face—the captain's trademark close-quarters center axis position. Both of his eyes were wide open and locked on Baldy-Tats.

The woman laughed, her tattoos shifting to black once more as she rapped a fist on her head. "You think that toy scares me? This skull's not stock anymore."

Cargo grinned wickedly. "Looks like a pulse pistol, doesn't it? Fools the guards on the sweep out there well enough too. I have nine programmable ballistic rounds in here. Right now, they're set to hollow-point, and you'll note that I'm aimed at your neck. I bet that fancy noggin of yours still needs blood to get up in it, right?"

"Put it down, pal" Whitey-Braid hissed.

Cheeky looked down to see Whitey-Braid holding a pistol on her, aimed low, up under her ribs. A focused pulse blast there could hit her heart and rip it apart.

"Jenn, how many times have I told you two fuck-heads that you're not welcome in here," Clarissa said from the door to the back room through which she and Cargo had disappeared. She held a kinetic rifle. Probably illegal on station, but apparently necessary at times.

"Clarissa!" Baldy-Tats chuckled. "Didn't know you were in today. Keeping the patrons busy, I see."

Cheeky realized that Cargo wasn't wearing a shirt—and seemed to have dinosaur underwear.

"Dino day?" she asked.

"Shut up, Cheeky," Cargo grumbled.

"Time to go, bitches," Clarissa said.

Whitey-Braid looked up at Baldy-Tats, and Cheeky suspected they were discussing options over the link.

"Nope!" Baldy-Tats shouted as she fell backward, her arm still wrapped around Cheeky, pulling them both to the ground as a shot rang out.

It sounded like Cargo's weapon, and Cheeky couldn't believe that he would fire with her that close.

As they fell to the ground, Cheeky twisted and landed facing Baldy-Tats. Above them, Clarissa's kinetic rifle boomed and Whitey-Braids—at least Cheeky suspected it was Whitey-Braids—screamed.

Baldy-Tats was bringing her pistol up to fire into Cheeky's abdomen, but this wasn't Cheeky's first bar fight, and it sure as hell wasn't going to be her last. She rose up and twisted to the side, narrowly avoiding Baldy-Tats's shot, while rising up and drawing both arms back.

She swung them down, while letting her body fall, adding to the force of the strike. The fingers on her right hand were folded at the first knuckle and that hand struck Baldy-Tats's throat.

The fingers on her left arm were extended, long nails flashing as they drove into the bald woman's right eye.

Baldy-Tats gave a gargled shriek, and Cheeky pulled her right arm back, driving her knuckles into Baldy-Tats's throat three more times until a strong hand caught Cheeky's wrist and pulled her up off the other woman.

"Stop!" Cargo shouted.

Cheeky looked down and saw Baldy-Tats, one artificial eye dangling free on her cheek, and both hands clawing at her crushed throat, desperate for air.

Then a sucking gasp came from the woman, and Cheeky realized that Baldy-Tats's armor must have punctured her lungs, directly feeding them air.

Her one eye was filled with a mixture of rage and awe, and she reached up to cup her other eye while struggling to her feet.

Cheeky turned to see Whitey-Braid bent over a chair, her armor cracked across the chest and blood seeping through.

"Last chance," Clarissa spat out. "Now *go*!"

Baldy-Tats grabbed Whitey-Briad under the arms and the women slowly limped out of the bar—which contained far fewer patrons than it had a minute earlier.

"And only come back if you want to fucking die!" Clarissa called out before turning to Cargo and Cheeky. "Aren't you two just a ton of fun. Station security will be here in five. Get your clothes and get out the back."

She stepped toward Cargo, wrapped an arm around him—at which point Cheeky realized that Clarissa was naked—and planted a kiss on his lips.

"Come back some time. We can do *that* again for free. Now give me your pistol. I don't have video in here, but they'll have audio of it firing, and I'll need to say that it's mine."

"You going to be OK with the cops?" Cargo asked.

"Yeah, it's fine. I have a license for heavier weapons in here. Station is cool with it because it means they don't have to patrol as much."

Cargo nodded and gave Clarissa a final longing look before he turned and gestured for Cheeky to follow him.

"You going to be OK?" Cheeky asked Clarissa. "Will they come back for you?"

Clarissa shook her head. "Those two have just worn out their welcome on Hermes Station. RHY has cleaned this place up a lot lately—they don't tolerate that sort of shit anymore."

"Good for something at least, then," Cheeky said as she followed Cargo to the rear door.

"Maybe," Clarissa replied with a grunt.

"Well, thanks anyway," Cheeky said, stepping into the back room—a storeroom with a cot against one wall.

"Cargo…seriously. Dino shorts. We have to talk about this."

RETYNA GIRL

STELLAR DATE: 09.03.8938 (Adjusted Years)
LOCATION: Hermes Station
REGION: Naga System, Orion Freedom Alliance Space

After waking and having a light breakfast, Jessica was led down a series of corridors to a large room filled with various props and a set of a-grav units—probably to simulate her flying.

Phoebe was waiting with a steaming cup of coffee, and let out a delighted gasp when she saw Jessica.

"Oh wow! They said you glowed, but I thought it would just be a little bit—shit, you look amazing. How does it feel to be Retyna Girl?"

<*Here goes,*> Jessica said to Iris.

<*You got this,*> Iris replied, sending supportive feelings into Jessica's mind.

"*Feel* to be Retyna Girl?" Jessica asked. "I *am* Retyna Girl."

Phoebe's smile grew into a broad grin. "Now that's what I want to hear. Let's get started."

The next few hours were spent with Jessica taking thousands of still images in a variety of outfits, reciting lines, and doing action stunts, flying about, and providing full range motion capture—in case they decided to make sims at some point.

Part way through the day, Trevor arrived and sat along one side of the room—where the food and beverages were arrayed—and watched with admiring eyes. He seemed to especially like the skimpy outfits they had put her in—the better to show off her glowing skin.

After her confession to Iris the night before, and her acceptance that this was a necessary sacrifice for her crew—

her family—she allowed herself to fully slip into the character of Retyna Girl, enjoying the release of being someone else.

"With Retyna Girl, light is never the enemy!" she cried out with a glowing fist thrust in the air, finally not giggling after the fifth try.

<*Nice to do something that's not super-serious-life-or-death for once, isn't it?*> Iris asked part-way through the day.

<*It really is,*> Jessica replied, smiling for the sensory capture devices.

As the day drew to a close, and the retakes had been completed, Jessica slipped away from the capture devices and approached Trevor.

"Looks like I'm done," she said as they embraced.

"Too bad." Trevor grinned. "I think I could watch you do that stuff all day—of course I recorded what I was here for, so I can sample your best lines as needed."

Jessica laughed. "Yeah, I kinda suspected that would happen."

"You seem far more OK with all this today than I thought—glowing skin notwithstanding."

"I had a really good heart-to-heart with Iris last night…about some stuff that happened a long time ago. Stuff I'm finally ready to share with you too."

Trevor placed his hands on either side of her face and leaned into a kiss.

"Glad to hear it, love," he said when they finally separated. "Here. I brought some clothes for you, just in case."

"Thanks!" Jessica said. "I like this dress, but these heels are starting to kill my feet."

Trevor glanced down at her feet and laughed. "Well, I didn't bring any shoes, so you might be in those for a bit longer."

"Men." Jessica shook her head and grabbed the duffle from his hands. She pulled the heels off and walked barefoot to the changing partition, knowing with absolute certainty that Trevor was watching her ass in the short, slinky dress she wore.

Once behind the partition, she slipped off the dress and opened the duffle. Within was her favorite purple shipsuit, and the unmistakable smell of new leather.

She reached in and pulled out the leather jacket, holding it up and examining the alterations. It looked perfect.

Jessica dressed quickly, and selected a lower pair of heels that she'd worn earlier in the day. She grabbed the empty duffle, and paused, eyeing the clothing from her multiple wardrobe changes during the shoot. With a quick glance to ensure no one was looking, she grabbed a few items—including the dress she had just been wearing and tossed them in the duffle.

Once her act of larceny was complete, she walked back out from behind the partition to be greeted by Trevor's wide smile.

She ran a hand down the jacket and returned the smile. *<It fits perfectly! Thanks for bringing it!>*

<A courier brought it just as I was leaving the ship. I figured you'd want to try it on,> Trevor replied.

<Well yeah,> Jessica laughed. *<Hey, Phoebe's back, I'm going to go ask when they're going to undo my glowyiness—though I kinda wish they didn't have to. I admit knowing it is coming from bacteria in my skin is a bit disconcerting.>*

<Bah, everyone's skin has bacteria in it. Though I'll admit, it's a good look on you. Either way Jess, you'll always be my Retyna Girl—I'll never fear the light!>

<You're going to be getting a lot of Retyna Girl lines tossed at you in the near future,> Iris laughed.

<Better believe it,> Jessica replied to Trevor with a wink.

She approached Phoebe, who was reviewing some of the capture with another woman.

"This was a lot of fun, Phoebe. I trust everything is in order now for our ship to scoop fuel?" Jessica asked.

Phoebe looked up and smiled brightly. "Just about, yup!"

"Right. I assume you first have to do the surgery to de-Retyna me?" Jessica asked.

Phoebe's diminutive features pinched as her brow furrowed. "Um, no, you're coming back to Bennia with me. You're Retyna Girl now."

Jessica took a step back, her eyes narrowing.

"We have a deal. One shoot, then you undo this, and we go our separate ways."

"Well yes, but there's a clause in the contract to extend your term indefinitely if everything goes well—which it did! You were great, Jessica. You're set for life now! A real superhero!"

Phoebe's face was glowing with excitement—either that or it was reflecting the light that seemed to be coming off Jessica more brightly as anger flooded her.

"We removed that clause. I specifically struck every clause that had to do with reappearances, reprisals, and anything of the like."

"Huh." Phoebe put a finger in her mouth. "I recall a discussion about that, but the version we have—one with your tokens on it—has all those clauses still in place and we're exercising them." The small woman's eyes narrowed as she reached up and put a hand on Jessica's cheek. "Don't worry. We'll take good care of you, Retyna Girl. Oh! By the way, I've started proceedings to have your name legally changed to that too! It's really awesome!"

Jessica couldn't tell if Phoebe thought that it was awesome, if she was putting on a show, or if maybe the diminutive woman was crazy.

<Iris…>

<I really have no freaking clue how they pulled that with the contract. It must have been some sort of MITM sleight of hand with the data routes.... The contract you put your tokens on is not the one we agreed to, or even the first one they presented you with. Holy crap...for all intents and purposes, they own you!>

<WHAT!?>

<Let me see what I can do...maybe I can hack in here and alter their records, put the right contract in place.>

<You better do that. Playing at Retyna Girl for a day was fun, but I have other things to do than cut ribbons at station openings and pose in the tiniest outfits they can find—not to mention prolonged exposure to Phoebe would probably make me want to punch her in the mouth. Repeatedly. Until she's dead.>

<Stall her.>

Jessica carefully schooled her expression—as much as she could. "Phoebe, I'm sure that Bennia is a great place, and being Retyna Girl would be a blast, but I have a crew, a family. I can't just leave them."

"You don't understand," Phoebe said, a look of worry clouding her face. "RHY Dynamics really wants Retyna to succeed. There's a lot of pressure, there are competing interests. You give us an edge. You're amazing. You're going to start a craze. We're going to drag Orion space into the future. Enough of this slow expansion, salt-of-the-earth stuff. RHY has the right people in the government to give us an edge. But we have to execute perfectly, and you're perfect—I'm not giving you up."

<This is insane, but insightful,> Jessica said to Iris before responding aloud to Phoebe in an acidic tone. "What's stopping me from just walking out of here?"

"Well, there's all the guards—we *are* deep within the RHY sector of the station." Phoebe winked at Jessica. "You're not *really* a superhero. You know that, right?"

<Oh shit, I just found something when I was breaching their network to swap contracts. Jessica, these people are serious baddies,> Iris interrupted suddenly. *<Play along for a minute.>*

Jessica sent an affirmative response to Iris and let her face fall. "No…so what now?"

Phoebe waved a hand in Trevor's direction. "Why don't you go say goodbye to your man-mountain over there and tell him to go get your things from your ship."

Jessica glanced at Trevor, and sighed. "Fine, but I'm getting a lawyer to undo this crazy contract."

Phoebe raised an eyebrow. "You did so well today, Retyna Girl. Don't make me do things you won't like to ensure your good behavior. I have a lot of shit to deal with—you're supposed to be a solution, not a problem."

Jessica decided that she'd pushed Phoebe far enough and let out an angry breath before turning and walking to Trevor.

<You don't look happy,> he said as she approached.

<Well, for starters, it looks like I'm a wholly owned subsidiary of RHY Dynamics,> Jessica sighed. *<Their contract gives me to them, mind, body, and soul for as long as they want it!>*

<Why'd you sign something like that?!> Trevor asked.

<Trevor! Seriously, I didn't. It's corporate BS.>

<Jessica, Trevor,> Iris said. *<None of that is important. These people are developing a serious bioweapon down on that planet for the OFA government.>*

<Seriously? Is it to use against the Transcend?> Trevor asked.

<How should I know? They don't exactly have their battle plans here,> Iris replied.

Jessica glanced back at Phoebe, who was still reviewing the results of the shoot. It was hard to believe that bubbly little waif was involved in something like this—although she may not know anything about it.

<So what are we going to do?> Jessica asked. *<We can't just let them develop this stuff—or take me off to Bennia for that matter.>*

<*Wait, take you where?*> Trevor asked.

<*Bennia. I guess it's where RHY is headquartered.*>

<*Well, ready to walk out of here and stop whatever nefarious plan these RHY guys have?*> Trevor asked.

<*Aren't you worried at all?*> Jessica asked.

<*About what? We just stood up against an entire TSF fleet and lived to tell the tale. What can these duffasses do to us?*>

<*It's worth noting that the TFS fleet was commanded by Finaeus's daughter, who really didn't want to kill us. These people are very unlikely to have familial connections,*> Iris countered.

<*I guess we should alert the crew and get back to* Sabrina,> Jessica said as she rolled her shoulders and raised each arm, stretching them out in preparation for the fight to come. <*So, shoot our way out of here and then stop their research, right?*>

<*Then we'd better get some guns to do all that shooting,*> Trevor said as he rose from his seat and grabbed a sausage roll from the food table.

DEPARTING

STELLAR DATE: 09.03.8938 (Adjusted Years)
LOCATION: Hermes Station
REGION: Naga System, Orion Freedom Alliance Space

<*Misha,*> Cheeky called the data dealer once more over the Link. <*Misha, where are you—you're five hours late!*>

She had been reaching out to him every fifteen minutes since he'd missed their prearranged meeting time at thirteen hundred hours. It was becoming more and more likely that Baldy—rather, Mandy and Jenn had caught up with him before they'd been booted off the station earlier in the day.

That had been fun to watch. Heavily armed station security had shown up at a local warehouse where the pair had been conducting some business—legitimate from the reports—and frog-marched the two women to their ship.

The pair's ship was only fifteen berths spinward on the docking ring and from *Sabrina*'s external cameras, they'd had a great view of a heavy tug latching on to Mandy and Jenn's ship—the *Endless Spark*—and hauling it off into space.

It had felt like sweet, sweet victory. Until Misha hadn't shown up.

"Any luck?" Cargo asked.

Cheeky shook her head. "I've got nothing. If he's on station, then he's disabled his Link."

"Well, I did manage to get some data on one good jump coreward. It's fifteen light years and takes us to a system where there's a few more people. Might be able to try our luck there."

Finaeus spoke up from the rear of the bridge. "It's not that hard to blind-jump across space—especially if you are going into well-travelled systems. The jump points out of this system, all have their available destinations broadcast on the beacons. We just jump toward the one that looks best."

"Except we don't know where to come out," Cheeky said. "Vector is one thing, but where do you drop from the DL?"

"Easy. You do it early." Finaeus shrugged. "Then you wait for another ship to pop out ahead, and then go back into FTL and hop to where they emerged."

Cargo shook his head slowly. "Yeah, that's possible. But it will add weeks to every single jump. I'm not exactly keen on the idea."

"True." Finaeus nodded. "It would add considerably to our travel time."

"Really, Cargo? Keen?" Cheeky asked.

<*Just got an encrypted message from Jessica,*> Sabrina interrupted. <*It's a doozy. Seems like Retyna pulled a switcheroo on her and she's now the property of RHY Dynamics. Oh, and they're also making a weaponized microbe capable of destroying the biospheres of enemy planets for the Orion government.*>

"Oh? Is that all?" Cargo asked, his voice dripping with sarcasm. "The more we travel to different stars, the more they're all the same."

"Well, I doubt you've encountered something like this before," Finaeus said, shaking his head. "I gotta say though, I'm surprised. Planet-killing biowarfare is really not Praetor Kirkland's MO."

"Well, it's someone's MO," Cheeky replied.

"Looks like Jessica wants to destroy their research labs on the station," Cargo said. "And Iris has identified their main facility on the planet below. She wants to take it out too and then get the heck out of dodge."

<*If she blows up RHY's labs on the spire, she stands zero chance of getting back through the station to our berth. You saw the heavies station security has.*> Hank said. <*We need to meet her somewhere in the middle.*>

"Trevor's with her, right?" Cheeky asked. "If someone could run them some weapons…"

"Run through the station with armfuls of heavy weapons?" Finaeus asked. "That's a bit on the nuts side. You'd be in a fight with station security in no time."

<RHY has a dock up there on the spire,> Sabrina offered. *<We can meet them at it.>*

<Going to have to time it right,> Hank replied. *<We can't just undock and float around waiting for them. Stations aren't usually keen on that.>*

"You too, Hank? Keen?" Cheeky laughed.

<Damnit, Cargo, now look what you've done to me,> Hank groused.

"You're welcome, Hank," Cargo said with a grin. "Unless someone has a better plan, that's what we're going with."

"OK. I'll get us in the departure queue," Cheeky said. "That's gonna determine our timing more than anything."

BREAKOUT

STELLAR DATE: 09.03.8938 (Adjusted Years)
LOCATION: Hermes Station
REGION: Naga System, Orion Freedom Alliance Space

<*Sabrina got the message,*> Iris reported. <*There's a dock up here on the spire that they want us to get to. They're in the docking queue now. It'll be forty-five minutes before they can pick us up.*>

<*A lot can happen in forty-five minutes,*> Trevor replied. <*The labs are only ten minutes from here, tops.*>

<*Dock's probably another fifteen from what I've seen of the layout up here.*> Jessica added. <*Give or take ten minutes to blow the lab and we're sitting on an extra twenty minutes.*>

<*A lot can happen in twenty minutes.*> Trevor said.

<*You're recycling your lines,*> Jessica sighed while glancing over at Phoebe who was involved in an animated conversation with one of her flunkies. Jessica was disliking that bubbly little woman more by the minute. <*You know…this would work a lot better with a hostage.*>

<*And what about the guards?*> Iris asked. <*Since Phoebe made her little revelation to you, a pair has shown up at every exit.*>

<*Easy,*> Jessica said with a smile. <*I gotta pee.*>

Trevor was still picking through the food on the services table while Jessica walked toward the nearest exit, not slowing as she approached a lightly-armored man and woman standing on either side of the door.

When one, the woman, stepped in front of her, Jessica stopped short, a look of surprise on her face.

"Excuuuse me?" She gave the woman her best entitled whine. "Out of my way."

<*Wow, that does not suit you—well, it does, but almost too well. Never do it again,*> Iris said.

<*Too late, I'm in character now.*>

"Sorry, we're under orders to keep you here," the woman—Kelly according to the name on her armor—replied.

"Do you see a can in here?" Jessica said in her best nasally voice, one that annoyed even her. "I really gotta peeeeee."

She watched Kelly look at Phoebe, and then her eyes darted to the right, the woman's Link-tell.

Jessica turned and saw Phoebe nod slowly. She smiled brightly in thanks and turned back to the guard.

<*You're overselling it,*> Iris said.

<*I dunno…I think Phoebe really is just an airhead with delusions of grandeur.*>

<*Just be careful. Both our asses are on the line.*>

<*Iris, this ass here is all mine.*>

<*Always have to ruin the metaphor.*>

"Follow me," Kelly said, and turned down the hall. Jessica fell in behind her, with the other guard trailing after.

The restrooms weren't far, and when the guards came in with her, Jessica laughed. "Curious to see if my piss glows too?"

"A bit." The man laughed as he walked through the entrance. "Is it purple, too?"

The woman elbowed him. "Shut up, Rand."

With a casual stealth few would expect from a man his size, Trevor slipped into the rest room and grabbed Rand by the head, lifting him bodily.

"Yeah, Rand, shut up. That's my lady you're talking about there."

Trevor threw the guard into the row of stalls while Jessica took advantage of the distraction to deliver a strike to the base of Kelly's skull. She cried out and spun to face Jessica. "Fucking bitch!"

"Both of those things are often true," Jessica said with a grin that disappeared as Kelly drew her pulse pistol and fired.

Jessica dove out of the way, only taking a small amount of force from the edge of the pulse wave.

Kelly turned to Trevor and fired a shot at him, which he shrugged off. He rushed the guard and drove a massive fist down on her head, then sunk another into Kelly's stomach.

She fell to the ground like a sack of potatoes and Trevor bent over her. "Shit, I think I broke her neck."

"I still read a heartbeat," Jessica said as she picked up the pulse pistol and waited for Iris to disable its bio-lock.

<*Safe,*> Iris announced as Rand began to disentangle himself from the wreckage of the stalls.

"Hey Rand, you guys should get your bosses to spring for better armor," Jessica said as she approached. "Or at least full helmets."

The man's eyes widened with fear as Jessica fired a pulse blast into his face.

"These two are going to be looking for a new job tomorrow." Trevor chuckled. "Well, maybe not tomorrow."

Jessica eyed the guards' armor. "No way either of us can fit into that. We'll just have to walk to the labs like we belong here and hope no one stops to question Retyna Girl and her entourage."

"Entourage of one, eh?" Trevor chuckled. "You're gonna have to work on your fan base."

"You know," Jessica said as she cracked the door open and peered out into the hall while Trevor stuffed the guard's rifles into the duffel, "if it wasn't for this whole pending war between Orion and the Transcend, I could maybe see myself getting into acting. It was kinda fun."

"Might need to figure out how to undo the glowyness—which would honestly make me kinda sad," Trevor said as they stepped out into the hall. "Probably not a lot of roles calling for glowing purple women."

<Oh, I know how to turn it off now,> Iris said. *<The microbes bleed off energy if it's not being consumed. I've been adding a new latticework in your skin to draw the charge off evenly. Once it's done, I can use the energy more efficiently, and that will diminish the glow.>*

"Good, because I'm starting to feel like a fucking lightbulb," Jessica said.

"And never was there a sexier light bulb," Trevor commented.

Jessica laughed. "That's a weak one, Trevor. Light bulbs aren't known to be sexy to begin with."

"Hey, they can't all be winners."

The Retyna Girl shoot had taken them toward the end of the station's second shift and they passed only a few RHY employees as they walked through the corridors.

Those they did pass gave her appreciative looks, and not a few open-mouthed stares. Almost all of them kept to the far side of the corridor as they passed.

<In the Inner Stars glowing people aren't that uncommon,> Jessica said. *<Heck, Sirius had a whole cult culture based around glowing.>*

<Yeah, but all these people know ***why*** *you're glowing,>* Trevor chuckled. *<And it seems like not all of them think it's a good thing.>*

<I kinda noticed that too,> Jessica replied.

<Regarding your new microbial friends…I think I can weaponize them,> Iris mused.

<Oh yeah?> Jessica asked. *<Not a bioweapon, though, right? That would be gross.>*

<No, not like that at all. Once I have the conductive latticework in your skin, I could direct the charge anywhere, not just into your SC Batts. It would probably be easiest to run larger conductors to your hands. Then you could electrocute people by touching them,> Iris said.

<I've seen people with that type of mod before,> Jessica said as she sent a passel of nanoprobes ahead to scout around the next intersection. *<But it usually kills their batts fast. How will these microbes have the charge to do any serious damage?>*

<That's the thing,> Iris said with a smile. *<The insulating properties of the polymers in your skin have turned each bacterial colony into amazing little batteries. They hold a wallop of a charge, maybe even as much as one joule per colony.>*

<Microbes, Iris, not bacteria. I know it's the same thing, but the thought of bacterial colonies in my skin is somewhat disconcerting,> Jessica said, cringing.

<Jessica, dear, you're an organic. Bacteria outnumber cells in your body ten to one. You're like one big petri dish.>

<Yeah, I know, but those bacteria aren't alien. So, how many colonies are there?>

<About a million, give or take a bit,> Iris replied.

<Holy shit, that's a million joules of energy!> Trevor exclaimed. *<Sounds like Retyna Girl just got a new super power.>*

<Well, that's a full discharge,> Iris cautioned. *<The cool thing is that because the power is stored chemically until drawn on, you don't look like a giant ball of EM energy walking around—well, you do glow on pretty much every spectrum, but it belies how much energy you actually have.>*

<How long does it take to recharge?> Jessica asked, looking down at her glowing hand.

<Not sure. Might be as long as an hour if you fully discharge.>

<I don't know if I'm more excited, or creeped out by this,> Jessica said.

Trevor chuckled. *<Well I'm a little turned on by it. You just get more bad-ass by the day.>*

<Seriously?>

<Oh c'mon, Jess, you're a sexy, glowing, lightning-charged superhero woman. If you could actually fly, I'd probably take you right here.>

Jessica laughed aloud. <*Easy now, big guy.*>

<*Jess does have wide enough hips that I bet we could mount a-grav systems in them. Might alter your range of motion though,*> Iris mused. <*Never mind with your waist, there's nowhere to put the extra SC Batts.*>

<*Can we focus on the mission?*> Jessica asked. <*You know the one where we have to stop the evil corporation from creating a biological super weapon that will wipe out all life in the galaxy if it runs rampant?*>

<*I suppose, but I'm still gonna ogle you a bit more while we do it,*> Trevor chuckled.

Jessica punched him in the arm. An action that probably hurt *her* more than him. <*You're incorrigible.*>

Trevor rubbed his arm, giving her a hurt look. Jessica shook her head in response, gestured at her eyes with two fingers, and then pointed down the hall.

<*Because that's not inconspicuous,*> Iris said.

Jessica recognized the area they were walking through. They'd been here the night before. She and Trevor were approaching the labs where she'd seen the automatons managing cultures. If she had to guess the one area in the facility where the dangerous stuff would be handled, Jessica would put her money on the labs where no humans ventured.

However, entering labs where only robots worked was not something on her bucket list, and Jessica kept walking, heading toward the areas where human technicians worked.

<*Ahead. The one on the left,*> Iris interrupted. <*Last night I saw some tanks in the back when someone opened the door as we passed. I don't recognize all their symbols here yet, but I think I spotted the chemical formula for methane.*>

Jessica replied with a mental nod and approached the door. She tugged gently, but it was locked. She casually leaned against the wall, and placed her hand on the access panel, feeling the tingle of nano passing through her skin. It felt different, more concentrated, and she realized that Iris must be routing it around the microbe colonies.

<*Amateur hour, here,*> Iris commented. <*Though probably sufficient to guard against the level of tech we've seen so far on station.*>

<*Plus, we're inside their perimeter,*> Trevor added. <*Though I suppose that's sloppy too.*>

<*OK, go,*> Iris said.

Jessica drew the pulse pistol she had taken from Kelly in the restroom and kicked open the door. There were seven people working in the room, and she opened fire on the three to her right, while Trevor hit the targets on the left.

It was nice working with someone for so long. After a while the tactics just came naturally, with no need to discuss who was covering what angle.

Jessica rushed around a table, and checked over the prone figures.

"Clear," she announced.

Trevor fired another shot at a man on the floor. "All set here."

"So," Jessica said. "They apparently don't have cameras in bathrooms, but they probably do in here. I bet we have thirty seconds."

<*Well, those tanks are indeed filled with methane, and there are some lovely oxygen tanks over there too,*> Iris said with a mental smile. <*Let's get to work.*>

LATE ARRIVAL

STELLAR DATE: 09.03.8938 (Adjusted Years)
LOCATION: Hermes Station
REGION: Naga System, Orion Freedom Alliance Space

Nance was securing a load in one of the starboard holds, when Cargo called down.

<Nance, Cheeky got us bumped in the queue. We're t-minus five to pull out from the station.>

<What? No! I'm not ready down here. I just got this last shipment situated, but it's not secured yet. Stars, where's Trevor when you need him?>

<What took so long?> Cargo asked.

<Oh, I don't know, maybe the fact that I took a batch of that Retyna stuff—like a crazy person, I might add—and I had to shift half my biomass around to get an isolated tank to put it in. Took all morning just to do that.>

Nance gestured to the cargo-bot hovering nearby to hold down the security net on the far side of a stack of crates while she locked her corner into the anchors.

<I'm sending Finaeus down to help,> Cargo replied

Great, I'm sure he'll be waaaay better than the cargo-bot, Nance thought to herself before responding, *<Kay, thanks.>*

Nance had hooked on two more corners of the safety net when Sabrina called out on the shipnet.

<There's a guy at the airlock. He's dancing around like he has to pee, demanding to see Cheeky.>

<Oh!> Cheeky exclaimed. *<That's Misha!>*

<Better late than never,> Cargo replied. *<Nance, go get him in. Finaeus can secure the cargo.>*

<Yeah, sure, send the old man to do the manual labor,> Finaeus groused.

<Are we really gonna take him with us?> Nance asked.

<It was a part of his deal. Based on how scared he looks, I bet he's running from more people than just Mandy and Jenn,> Cargo replied. *<Let him in and make sure he's got the maps, Nance.>*

<Fine,> Nance replied, and told the cargo bot to stay before running out of the hold.

She passed Finaeus amidships and called out as she passed. "Secure the last three stacks, then the bot, and sweep the other holds for anything unsecured."

"Sure thing, Mom," Finaeus called over his shoulder.

<Just when he was starting to grow on me,> Nance said privately to Erin.

<He's OK, just old and eccentric. Just think how weird you'll be when your neural pathways are several thousand years old.>

<Erin! That's not nice at all!>

<Sorry, I thought it was funny. AI humor often doesn't translate well. Most of the words we have for organics don't have good analogies.>

Nance laughed aloud. *<I'll bet they don't.>*

She reached the airlock, and paused to watch as the station-side lock slid open on the holodisplay above the main bay's doors. Misha rushed in and pressed himself against *Sabrina*'s outer lock as pulse blasts rippled through the air out on the sweep.

With a wave of her hand, she triggered the main bay's lock to open and Misha fell in. As the door closed once more, a pulse blast slipped through and clipped Misha in the shoulder.

"Shit," Nance muttered and signaled the station's portal to close and save *Sabrina* from taking any more fire.

She sent a command for the station's lock to close, but the command was rejected. The station-side lock remained wide open.

Several figures in mismatched armor appeared on the feeds, four continued to fire pulse blasts, while a fifth set down a case and began pulling out the components for a railgun.

<*We're taking pulse weapon fire,*> she announced over the shipnet. <*Which is about to get a lot worse. So much for station security.*>

<*Noticed that,*> Cargo replied. <*Wait! Is that a railgun?!*>

<*Yeah, and the station side lock isn't closing. We need to get out of here, but if we pull off we'll decompress the dock.*>

<*They must have ES shields,*> Cheeky said. <*I'm sure it will be fine.*>

<*Except that Hermes Station won't take it as fine and our chances of making it to the spire without coming under fire will be zero,*> Erin said.

<*I can hack the station's door controls through the comm hookup,*> Nance said. <*I think.*>

<*You've been getting good at breaking encryption,*> Erin said. <*Not as good as Iris, yet, but I'm really impressed.*>

<*Great,*> Nance replied as she sent a flood of packets at the station's control system, looking for a vulnerable port. <*Can you deal with that Misha guy? He seems to be freaking out in there. Oh, and make him put on one of the hazsuits. Who knows what's crawling all over him.*>

<*You got it,*> Erin replied with a mental smile.

As she worked, Nance glanced at the video feed on her HUD to see Misha reluctantly stripping and allowing the airlock to run its sanitizing cycle.

<*Hah, look at that, they did leave a port open,*> Nance said. <*Of course, I can't follow their architecture…it's like a foreign language.*>

She reached up to run a hand through her hair and hit the helmet of her hazsuit. Why was she wearing this stupid thing anyway? The nano she had received on the *Intrepid* offered more protection than any suit.

Old habits die hard, I guess.

She rolled her head, stretching out a kink, and saw that the man with the railgun was nearly done assembling it. And now another appeared to be holding a detpack.

<*Any ideas on this architecture? Erin?*>

<*I think it's based on an old Scattered Disk setup,*> Erin said. <*Send it this packet and it'll think it's exposed to vacuum and it will shut. I hope.*>

The first few rounds from the railgun hit *Sabrina*'s outer airlock. The ablative plating chipped and dented, but so far held.

<*Thanks,*> Nance said and sent the packet through the opened port.

The station-side airlock flashed a warning light, and a decompression announcement passed over the station's general net a moment before the doors slammed shut, narrowly avoiding the man with the detpack.

<*Holy shit, that was close,*> Nance said with a gasp.

<*Uh…still is. He dropped the detpack. It's sitting on the deck between us and the station,*> Erin replied.

<*You hear that up there?*> Nance called to the bridge. <*We gotta go, now!*>

As she spoke, the inner lock opened, and Misha rushed in, hazsuit on, though the seal on his helmet wasn't matched properly.

"Shit, you guys gotta go, those asshats have a ship and they're mad enough to shoot!" he yelled as he ran toward Nance who stepped back.

"Seal your helmet! That station is crawling with Retyna germs!"

"What? Fine, but you have to go!" Misha yelled.

Nance watched the man re-seat the hazsuit's helmet before approaching him. "Follow me. We're almost undocked."

<*Twenty seconds,*> Cheeky announced.

<We better hope the timer on that detpack is long,> Erin said. *<If it goes off in that enclosed space…>*

<There's another ship requesting emergency undock,> Cargo said. *<The* Undulating Fire. *Friends of yours, Misha?>*

<Uhhhh…until recently, yes.>

<You bring the maps?> Cheeky asked. *<Because we're gonna need them.>*

<Yeah, I have them, just get me out of here and they're all yours.>

Nance led Misha through the central passageway toward the ladders. *<All in good time, we have another rescue to perform first.>*

KABOOM

STELLAR DATE: 09.03.8938 (Adjusted Years)
LOCATION: Hermes Station
REGION: Naga System, Orion Freedom Alliance Space

By some miracle, only two guards appeared within the first few minutes after they'd entered the lab. Trevor let them get inside before taking each one out. They had put up more of a fight and now their lifeless bodies lay just within the entrance.

"OK, we're all set," Jessica announced as she examined the improvised incendiary she had crafted. "Dump the lab techs in the corridor and give 'em a kick in the ass, should wake 'em up."

"How are we going to make sure that no one comes in here and disarms your explosive?" Trevor asked as he hauled two of the unconscious techs out into the corridor—much to the shock of a man passing by in the corridor. "Food poisoning. Did you have the chicken in the commissary?"

The man blanched. "Uh...yeah..."

"Shit man, get to the infirmary, *fast*!" Trevor bellowed and the man took off running. "Heh. Works every time."

<Regarding the explosives, I think that I can seal the door, and then trigger a biocontaminant alert. That should take them some time to shut down, it should also clear the area out,> Iris offered.

"Almost sounds too easy," Jessica said as she rose from setting her device and opened up the valves on the tanks, taking care to get the right mixture for explosive combustion. "Let's go, this is going to get toxic fast."

She strode to the lab's entrance and watched as Trevor slapped one of the techs. "C'mon buddy, time to wake up and run for your life."

"Wha?" the man asked as pulse shots erupted from a cross-corridor twenty meters to their left.

Jessica turned to see a half-dozen RHY security guards rushing down the passageway. The man Trevor was holding saw them as well, and was on his feet seconds later, running down the opposite end of the hall.

Trevor, on the other hand, shouldered his pulse rifle and raced toward the approaching guards, firing wildly and screaming at the top of his lungs.

The guards were unprepared for the hundreds of kilos of man-mountain rushing toward them and several stopped shooting, their mouths hanging agape.

Two were felled by Trevor's pulse blasts, and then he crashed into two more. Jessica followed after him, firing on the final two guards, catching one in the face with pulse blasts that bowled him over. The other leveled his rifle at Jessica and fired a concentrated pulse at her. Jessica raised her arms reflexively, and felt a strange sensation in the palms of her hands. And then the bone-numbing force of a pulse wave—which she'd been dreading—never arrived.

"What the hell?" she asked, looking at her hands.

<Sorry, didn't have time to ask you if it was OK. I emitted a piezo-electric pulse through your hands, it nullified the pulse wave.>

Trevor smashed a fist into the man who had fired on Jessica, before raising a hand to massage his jaw. "That would sure be handy—no pun intended. Pulse blasts hurt like a bitch."

An alarm wailed around them, and a blast door began to lower a dozen meters down the hall.

<Go! Go!> Iris cried out. *<They've triggered the biocontaminant alerts to try and trap you in here.>*

<Hey, that was our plan!> Jessica replied.

<I hope in our version we were supposed to be on the other side of the door,> Trevor said.

Jessica took off running, Trevor close on her heels. They reached the door and slid under it a moment before it closed, Trevor clipping his ear on the door's seal.

"Fuck! Ow!" he swore as he gingerly touched his ear.

"Still attached," Jessica said as she glanced up at him. "Let's move."

<*Still, it **was** nice of them to seal off the section for us back there,*> Iris said. <*I've added a bit of my magic to the mix and it'll take them a bit longer to get the doors back open.*>

"Good work," Jessica replied as they dashed down the corridor, taking a right at an intersection as they angled toward where they suspected the RHY docks on the spire to be.

Jessica was in the lead, and passed into an area filled with doors leading off to private offices. They were outpacing her nanoprobes and she prayed that the way ahead was clear when a door ahead opened. Soldiers in heavy armor spilled out, weapons leveled at the pair. Jessica skidded to a halt, ready to beat a hasty retreat when she saw more soldiers file out of two offices behind them.

"Kinetics. We can't take that kind of firepower," Trevor said as he lowered his rifle.

"Well, this sucks," Jessica said as she followed suit.

"For you, yeah." Phoebe's voice came from beyond the soldiers, followed by the appearance of the woman herself a moment later. "I'm not letting you get away so easily. When we get you to Bennia, I'll have you fitted with a compliance chip and this will get a lot easier." She glanced at Trevor. "Maybe him too. I bet he'd make a good personal guard for Retyna Girl once she starts making all of her promotional appearances."

"Weapons on the ground. All of them," one of the soldiers said as he approached the pair. "Duffel too. Kick it over."

Jessica let out a long sigh and complied. Trevor dropped his as well and chuckled.

"Looks like you're going to get that career change after all," he said.

"Take them to my ship, and put them in stasis," Phoebe ordered the soldiers. "And sweep the corridors back there, find out what they were up to."

One of the guards unzipped the duffel and rifled through it. "Just clothes," he said.

Phoebe laughed. "Look at you, making off with all of Retyna Girl's gear. I knew you wanted to be her."

Jessica laughed. "What can I say. I'm a sucker for purple."

BLAST OFF

STELLAR DATE: 09.03.8938 (Adjusted Years)
LOCATION: Hermes Station
REGION: Naga System, Orion Freedom Alliance Space

"Clamps released. Pushing off on grav drive," Cheeky announced.

"Gonna piss them off." Cargo sighed.

"Better than that detpack going off while we're cheek by jowl with the station," Cheeky replied.

"Oh, I know. Cargo chuckled. "I was just lamenting it nonetheless."

Cheeky opened up the ship's grav thrusters and eased them away from the station. Past the ten-meter mark, then twenty…forty…seventy…one-hundred….

<Explosion aft,> Sabrina announced. *<I deflected it with conventional shields. Damn, it really dented the station something serious. They're leaking atmo.>*

"Shit, they're gonna blame us for this," Cargo muttered.

<Call from the Dockmaster's office,> Sabrina said. *<They're about as happy as you'd expect.>*

"Put 'em on," Cargo ordered.

A moment later, a woman appeared on the bridge's main holo, already yelling before the holo fully materialized. "—fuck do you think you're doing? Grav drives, shooting at the station! Cease acceleration *immediately!* We're bringing our turrets online!"

"Dockmaster Jera," Cargo replied in his calmest voice. "We were under attack from unknown assailants dockside. They had explosives and we needed to open up space for the blast to dissipate. If we hadn't it would have done a lot worse than crack a few seals on your airlock."

"Assailants?" Dockmaster Jera asked, looking away for a moment. "I do have reports of fighting on the dock near your berth." She frowned and shook her head. "Either way, you need to cease acceleration and hold your course. We're sending out a patrol craft to board you—we have reason to believe you have a fugitive aboard."

"Fugitive?" Cargo asked.

"Yes, one Misha Cairns. We have vid of him entering your ship right before you broke free from the station."

"We did bring him aboard, yes," Cargo agreed. "He was being fired upon by those attackers. We had a meeting scheduled with him."

"*We'll* be the judge of all that. Our patrol craft will be locked on your vector in five, ready to dock in ten—what are you doing?"

The dockmaster disappeared from the holotank and Cheeky shot a look back at Cargo. "Heard enough, eh?"

"Yup. Nice find with that Misha guy. Hope he actually has those maps and wasn't just looking for a ride."

"Me too," Cheeky replied softly. "For his sake."

Cheeky continued to alter vector, turning *Sabrina* in a wide parabola, the system's star their apparent destination. However, that fiction would be shattered in six minutes when she would fire the fusion drives and boost toward the station's spire for their smash-and-grab pickup of Jessica and Trevor.

"Here's our guest," Nance said as she entered the bridge with Misha.

"Nice hazsuit," Cheeky said, stifling a laugh. Misha appeared to have put it on in a rush, and one of the arms was twisted once around and the boots weren't seated correctly.

"She wouldn't let me on without it—well, not her, someone named Erin."

<*That'd be me,*> Erin said over the general shipnet.

"Are you the ship's AI?" Misha asked, looking around.

<_No, **I'm** the ship's AI, Sabrina,_> Sabrina said.

<*Then who are you, Erin?*> Misha appeared perplexed.

<*I'm embedded with Nance.*>

Misha whistled. "Wow, two AI on a ship this small."

<*Five,*> Sabrina said, at the same moment that Piya said, <*Four.*>

<*Oh,*> Piya added. <*I was counting who was aboard right now, took it too literally.*>

"Shit, seriously?" Misha asked. "You have five AI on this tub?"

<*Hey!*> Sabrina said. <_This **tub** as you have so inconsiderately called me, has just saved your ass, with no small risk to our own._>

"That makes it sound like we collectively just have one ass," Cheeky said.

"Well, stars know that Cheeky has enough ass for three or four people," Finaeus said as he entered the bridge and took his customary seat.

"So, Misha," Cargo said while snapping his fingers to get Misha's attention. "Maps. Do you have the maps?"

"Yeah, I do. Once you honor your side of the deal."

"Honor our—" Nance said, taking a threatening step toward Misha.

Cargo stood as well. "We're going to give you a free ride far away from here—that your maps will help with—or we're gonna kick you out an airlock for whomever you've pissed off to find. Pick."

Misha didn't respond immediately, and Cargo took a step forward. "We've had a bit of hard luck lately, friend. We're being very accommodating, given the trouble you've brought down on us. Now, give us the maps."

"OK, OK, sheesh, so testy," Misha muttered. "There, I pushed the data onto your shipnet.

Cheeky looked them over, noting the absence of several obvious trade routes. Misha was probably holding back on them for later. Still it was enough to get them started on their journey.

"Looks good enough for now," she said.

"Nance, can you put him in one of the spare rooms for now?" Cargo asked.

"Sure," Nance nodded. "This way, pastry man."

"Well, I don't actually cook…not really," Misha said.

"What about the prep table and everything in your stall?" Cheeky asked.

"Convincing, wasn't it?" Misha grinned.

"Seriously, let's go," Nance said. "I have stuff to do that doesn't involve babysitting your ass."

"Fine. Hey, no need to push!"

SHIP TO BENNIA

STELLAR DATE: 09.03.8938 (Adjusted Years)
LOCATION: Hermes Station
REGION: Naga System, Orion Freedom Alliance Space

"I have to say, I admire your moxie," Phoebe said turning her head to look back at Jessica and Trevor. "Just like something I could imagine Retyna Girl doing. You're a lot tougher than you look."

"You have no idea," Jessica replied. "But you will."

"Oh yeah?" Phoebe asked. "How's that?"

<*Yeah,*> Iris asked privately. <*How **is** that?*>

<*The usual, wait for the right moment, overpower the guards, punch Phoebe in the head repeatedly, steal her ship.*>

"Thought so. All talk," Phoebe said, unaware of Jessica's conversation with Iris, turning forward once more.

<*I count fourteen guards,*> Iris said. <*That's a lot. Even for Retyna Girl.*>

<*What about my new powers?*> Jessica asked with a chuckle. <*I'll stop their pulse blasts, then lightning-bolt them.*>

<*Check this out,*> Iris said, pulling a new readout onto Jessica's HUD. <*This is the level of charge your microbes have, and how long it will take them to reach full charge.*>

<*I can't help but notice that it's purple...with the Retyna Girl logo on it,*> Jessica commented drolly.

<*Noticed that, did you?*> Iris passed a mental smile. <*I like to take pride in my work. Anyway, you'll see that you're at less than half charge—which I'm estimating, the microbes have not yet built up a full charge for me to properly calibrate the gauge.*>

<*So based on this rate of charge, it'll take another five minutes to be able to stop another pulse blast,*> Jessica said. <*I thought these things were super-efficient.*>

<They are—at converting mutispectrum light into energy. These hallways aren't well lit—not like being in full sunlight. Plus, you're wearing clothing that covers most of your skin. You're charging only on your face and hands.>

Jessica pulled down the slider on the front of her shipsuit, letting more of her chest show. She noticed Trevor glance down and smile.

<Planning on distracting the guards?> he asked.

<No. Charging my skin.>

Trevor laughed aloud, drawing looks from several of the guards. *<Our lives are so very far from normal.>*

"We can tell when you use the Link," one of the guards said. "Cut it out or we knock you out."

Jessica had suspected as much, which was why she was glad Trevor hadn't asked about her plans of escape. She wasn't worried about their captors breaking their encryption, but better safe than sorry.

Instead, she flickered the glow in her eyes, flashing a quick message that she hoped Trevor would pick up. It was simple: "We take their ship."

Trevor looked away and yawned, their signal for acknowledgement.

Several minutes later, they were led through a large airlock and into a wide bay. Jessica peered down its length, gauging the space to be roughly two hundred by five hundred meters. The spaceward side of the bay had its doors pulled wide, a grav shield holding the atmosphere within.

Beyond the doors, the light of the Naga System's star shone through, its yellow-blue glow striking Jessica with unfiltered intensity. She felt her skin tingle and its glow increase in the direct starlight. On her HUD, the RG power meter began to climb faster, crossing over the fifty percent mark.

<Feels good!> Jessica exclaimed. *<I wonder what full power will feel like?>*

<*Organics,*> Iris replied.

Ahead, several ships rested on cradles in the bay, and Phoebe led them toward a silver vessel with sleek lines.

<*Bonus,*> Jessica said to Iris. <*That thing's small. Not even fifty meters.*>

<*Not going to fit all these guards, that's for sure,*> Iris replied.

Phoebe walked up the lowered ramp and four guards escorted Jessica and Trevor onto the ship.

<*Think you can hack the ramp?*> Jessica asked.

<*Brush your hand across that control panel as you walk by,*> Iris said, highlighting a panel over Jessica's vision.

<*You got it.*>

Jessica touched the panel, and a passel of nano flowed out of her hand onto its surface.

Once at the top of the ramp, Phoebe turned left, and walked down a short passageway to a room with five stasis pods.

"Your man will be a tight fit, but I think we can squeeze him in. If not, we'll just dump him out the airlock," Phoebe said, chuckling.

"You're not nearly as nice as you like to pretend," Trevor said with a low growl.

"Me?" Phoebe squeaked. "I think I'm plenty nice. I grabbed your friend, plucked her from obscurity. I'm going to make her a star! All she has to do is play along and she'll be set for life—or for however long we run the Retyna Girl marketing campaign."

"You're all heart," Jessica said with a sour smile.

<*Got it!*> Iris announced. <*Ramp is closing!*>

Trevor turned to the guard on his left. "Hey, buddy, guess what?"

"What?" the guard asked.

Trevor twisted his arms around and a resounding *SNAP* filled the air. He pulled his hands from behind his back and held them up. "I broke my cuffs."

"Shit!" the guard yelled as one of Trevor's fists jabbed forward, smashing the man's nose.

Jessica pulled her hands free as well, relying on nano, not brute strength to get the cuffs open. One of the guards fired a pulse blast at her, and she held up her right hand, nullifying the concussive waves while grabbing the throat of another guard who had closed in too quickly, discharging the rest of her skin's energy.

The guard shrieked and collapsed.

"Shit, that's cool," Phoebe whispered as Jessica pulled up her right leg and pivoted while kicking high, catching the first guard under the jaw. His weapon flew into the air as he fell back. Jessica caught it, spun it around and drove the weapon's butt into his temple.

She turned to see Trevor dropping the final guard with a blow to the throat.

"Tangos down," Trevor grinned.

Jessica deployed a stream of nano to the rifle, disabling its biolock and turned back to Phoebe. "Yeah, I'm pretty fucking awesome, aren't I?"

"Who *are* you?" Phoebe asked, her eyes wide with awe.

"Phoebe, really?" Jessica smirked. "I'm Retyna Girl."

MEET UP

STELLAR DATE: 09.03.8938 (Adjusted Years)
LOCATION: Hermes Station
REGION: Naga System, Orion Freedom Alliance Space

<*That Jera lady is getting very upset,*> Sabrina said. <*She's disrupting my calm.*>

"Oh, and they've started firing at us," Cheeky said. "Nothing serious yet, just lasers. Our shields are diffusing them."

"Three patrol craft coming after us too," Cargo said. "I imagine that they'll up the ante before long."

"How are you going to stop at those docks for Jessica and Trevor to get aboard if you're under fire?" Finaeus asked.

Cheeky looked back at Cargo and Finaeus. "Honestly? I have no idea—other than using our stasis shields, but that kinda lets the cat out of the bag, doesn't it?"

"Just a bit," Finaeus agreed. "We'll have every ship this side of the Orion Arm gunning for us."

"Have you managed to reach our wayward crewmembers yet, Sabrina?" Cargo asked.

<*Not yet, no. They seem to be off the station network, but Erin and I did pull a report of fighting in the RHY sector of the spire, so I think we can assume that they're on their way.*>

"We could modulate our shields and slip through their grav barrier on the bay," Finaeus suggested.

"That never works," Cheeky replied. "You've been watching too many vids."

"And you seem to forget that I've created half the tech you use on a daily basis."

<*Half seems excessive,*> Piya said.

"Well, maybe a quarter…a tenth. But I've worked on, or enhanced a lot more. Let me see if I can detect the frequency their graviton emitters are using."

<*And plan B?*> Cargo asked Cheeky privately.

<*Hope they can get out of the bay so I can scoop them up like Jessica did for Finaeus and me?*> Cheeky suggested. <*But that requires us reaching out—Oh shit, those patrol craft are firing on us to now!*>

<*Shields holding,*> Sabrina replied. <*But that other ship that broke free from the station, the uh…*Undulating Fire. *It's closing too…not fast, though. They seem content to let the station's ships take us out.*>

"Sabrina, Erin, I need you to raise Jessica somehow. Letting them know our plan is cru—"

<*Hey, you guys were late, so we caught our own ride,*> Jessica's voice cut Cargo off. Cheeky flipped the main holo to show the bay on the station's spire. A small silver ship shot out into space, followed by a cloud of debris.

Turrets began tracking the ship's position, and Cheeky boosted, arcing toward the ship to provide covering fire.

<*Bringing our rails online,*> Sabrina said. <*Firing on the turrets.*>

"We knew you'd have something up your sleeve, Jessica." Cargo chuckled. "Got a plan for getting over here?"

"This thing is pretty tiny. Think we could fit it in the main bay?"

<*No way,*> Sabrina said. <*Not without tearing a few holes in both our hulls. But if you pull up underneath, we can use the cradle clamps to hold onto you.*>

<*Sounds like a plan, Sabs,*> Jessica replied. <*Cheeky, sling me a vector.*>

<*Sure thing, Jess. Just give me a second. I gotta say, you sound pretty chipper,*> Cheeky said with a smile on her lips.

<Hell yeah. I'm having a blast. Kicking ass in outer space, isn't that what the brochure said?>

<Trevor. Is she OK?> Cargo asked.

Trevor's laugh filled their minds. *<She's doing great. Just on a bit of a high at the moment. The sunlight is hitting her full-on through this ship's forward window and that seems to make her giddy.>*

"That's fascinating," Finaeus mused. "From the Retyna they covered your skin in?"

"Embedded in her skin, more like," Trevor said.

"Really?" Finaeus asked. "That's fascinating."

"You mentioned that already," Cargo said.

<Oh, and I glow now too!> Jessica added.

Cheeky whistled. "Now *that's* cool. I bet you look way sexy all glowing."

<You have no idea,> Jessica replied.

"Can you two be serious for a moment?" Cargo asked.

Cheeky twisted in her seat and gave Cargo a level look, before mouthing the words, 'SS Sexy'.

"Jessica, you have the vector?" Cargo asked, ignoring Cheeky.

<On it, jinking a bit to keep those turrets away, but looks like we can line up just past the station's southern spire.>

"Great," Cargo replied.

<Got two of 'em!> Sabrina called out. *<Kinda nice not having you around, Jessica. You always hog the guns in combat.>*

Jessica laughed. *<Sorry, Sabrina, I'll make sure to give you a turn next time.>*

"What about those patrol craft?" Finaeus asked.

"Trying not to kill too many people in this system," Cargo replied. "Got any non-lethal ideas?"

Finaeus stroked his jaw. "Do you have any nukes aboard?"

"Not sure how that fits the bill for non-lethal," Cargo said.

"Small, tactical, we just need an EMP blast, and enough of a deterrence for them to back off."

Cheeky reviewed the positions of the ships on Scan. Jessica's small vessel was thirty kilometers ahead of them, already beyond the station's spire, which *Sabrina* was now flying past. The patrol craft were fifty klicks behind, keeping their distance, holding their fire as they approached the station.

"Once we get past, they're really going to open up on us," Cheeky said as she dove around a structural support.

<Oh, that's when we just boost for the planet,> Jessica replied.

"We what?" Cargo asked, moments before Scan picked up a large explosion behind them.

"What was that?" Cheeky asked. "Is that other ship shooting at the station's ships?"

<No,> Jessica replied. *<That's the bomb we planted in RHY's labs. Glad to see they didn't disarm it in time.>*

"Lay it out, Jessica," Cargo ordered.

"You know how Finaeus and Nance were worried about alien microbes killing everyone? Well, RHY is working on a weaponized version to sell to the Orion government."

"Fuckers!" Finaeus spat. "We have agreements about shit like this. No biological planet-killing WMDs. We have to take that thing."

<Yeah, that's why we have to hit the planet,> Jessica said. *<I have the coordinates for their base. Once you grab hold of us, we'll need to fly down there and nuke it.>*

"Well, we just have two small tacnukes," Finaeus said. "Those aren't going to do it. We could hit it with all our kinetics."

<One small tacnuke,> Nance added. *<I'm modifying the other to drop behind like you suggested. I think the best point is fifty klicks after we pass the station's southern spire.>*

"Do it," Cargo said.

"I'll coordinate, Nance," Cheeky said. "Marker is set."

<*Shit, that's less than a minute!*> Nance exclaimed.

"Better get moving."

<*I'm in the pocket,*> Jessica said. <*Hit me, Cheeks.*>

<*My turn to swoop in and save* **your** *ass,*> Cheeky said with a laugh. A moment later a vibration resonated through the deck and Cheeky called out, "Clamps engaged. We've got them."

<*Dropping the nuke,*> Nance reported.

Cheeky brought up the three pursuing patrol craft on the main holotank. They were all within ten kilometers of one another—a perfect target. A moment later the nuke detonated, its flaring light attenuated by the holo. Then the blast splashed across their shields and Scan shut down from the EM disturbance. When it came back on, they saw the wave hit the station, lighting up its shields with plasma flares.

"Slowed our pursuers down?" Cargo asked.

"Maybe," Cheeky said, accepting his suggestion. "Too soon to tell—oh, yeah, one just killed their engines, we might have done some serious damage there. The other two are dropping back. I bet they don't get paid enough to deal with crazy nuke-dropping people like us."

"Yeah, but now Misha's other friends in the *Undulating Fire* are coming for us," Cargo said with a sigh.

<*Firing rails on them,*> Sabrina said. <*Let's see if they want to dance in the dark.*>

"Show 'em who's boss, Sabrina," Finaeus said with a chuckle. "By the way, I think we need to do something a bit more extreme to that planet down there."

"Oh yeah?" Cargo asked. "Like what?"

"Well, as best I can tell from Scan, the facility Jessica is sending us to isn't the only one. Sure, it may be the one making their bioweapon, but we don't know that it's the only one. I say we wipe the planet's surface clean."

"Whoa, hey, is that more of this 'kill all the aliens' shit?" Cheeky asked.

Finaeus shook his head. "That planet's a factory. They're going to manufacture their weaponized microbes at scale. Destroying research facilities will just slow them. We need to stop them. If we don't, trillions will die."

"Well, what are our options," Cargo asked.

"Do what you did to The Mark's fleet at Bollam's World," Finaeus said somberly. "Boost out around the moon, and slam this ship into that planet full force."

Cheeky turned in her seat to stare at Finaeus. "You're nuts! We'll get lodged in the planet's core! With that Mark fleet we had clear space on the far side to drift into."

"You'll have to go full stasis for the impact, and then pop out and boost hard. You'll have liquified the crust at the impact point, so it should be possible to get back out."

"Should!" Cargo said. "Should doesn't buy you much when it comes to smashing into planets."

"Are you sure we'll have enough energy?" Cheeky asked. "Even if we get up to $0.1c$ we can't deliver that much kinetic energy."

"It's about where we hit," Finaeus said. "That planet has a thin crust, if I can find the right fault line, we can fracture an entire continent. That should do the trick."

<We're coming over in EV suits,> Jessica said. *<If we're planet-bustin' we don't want to be strapped onto* Sabrina*'s belly.>*

<You just stay in that suit when you get aboard,> Nance cautioned. *<I don't want you shedding your microbes all over.>*

"Captain?" Cheeky asked. "Your orders?"

<I think we can do it,> Sabrina said. *<We struck that gas giant's upper atmosphere with almost as much force back at Bollam's World.>*

"OK." Cargo rubbed his eyes with the heels of his hands. "I'm not going to let worlds get turned into graveyards when we could have stopped it. But let me go on the record as saying that we need to get more nukes…or something…we can't just keep slamming into everything. One day we're gonna hit something that doesn't give."

"Laying in a course," Cheeky said.

The two patrol craft still in pursuit had backed off to a distance of five hundred kilometers, apparently content to simply let the ship filled with crazy people leave at this point—either that, or they were waiting for backup.

However, the *Undulating Fire* continued to trade shots with *Sabrina.*

<*Bastards aren't giving me much to hit,*> Sabrina said. <*What I wouldn't give for an RM right now. Fire one of those and forget about 'em.*>

Cheeky spooled out the AP drive's nozzle, grateful that they had managed to purchase a few grams of antihydrogen on Hermes Station before their expeditious departure.

She aimed *Sabrina*'s prow toward the planet's moon, Aresa, boosting toward its north pole. As she approached she rotated the ship, describing a tight arc around the grey barren surface, wondering for a moment if they were passing over any underground cattle farms. Once past the moon, Cheeky opened up the ship's engines to their full capacity, and lit the AP drive. They flashed past the L1 point between the moon and Marsalla, continuing to pick up speed as they raced toward the purple/green world growing larger in the forward view.

<*Well, at least this has shut the station up on comms,*> Sabrina said. <*They must not have a clue what we're doing.*>

"RMs on our tail!" Cheeky called out.

<*Damnit, see! We need RMs!*> Sabrina said.

"On it," Cargo replied, firing countermeasures behind the ship, and activating point defense beams.

<*At least the RMs got the* Undulating Fire *to back off, almost like having our own,*> Sabrina added.

"Hey guys," Jessica announced as she raced onto the bridge.

"Holy shit, you *do* glow!" Finaeus said, amusement and wonder in his voice.

"What happened to keeping your EV suit on?" Cargo asked.

"It's fine," Jessica replied as she slid into her seat "Iris is certain that I'm safe to be around."

<*We'll talk about this later,*> Nance said, her tone ominous.

"Sure, Nance, if we survive destroying a planet, we can talk about how I got turned into a glowing superhero to satisfy some debutante's need for a catchy marketing campaign," Jessica shot back.

"Jessica, stop those RMs from blowing us up first," Cargo ordered. "Then we'll worry about the planet."

"Oh, crap, RMs! Missed that on my rush up here."

MARSALLA

STELLAR DATE: 09.03.8938 (Adjusted Years)
LOCATION: Hermes Station
REGION: Naga System, Orion Freedom Alliance Space

Jessica adjusted Scan resolution and examined the pair of relativistic missiles pursuing *Sabrina*. Correction, near-relativistic missiles. They were still under 0.6*c*, but even at that velocity they'd be kissing *Sabrina*'s hull in less than thirty seconds.

She saw that Cargo had already deployed chaff to no effect. She turned the beams on the missiles, but they were jinking too much, and Jessica knew any hit would be a lucky one.

"Priming the rails with grapeshot," she announced.

"No way you can hit them with that," Cargo said.

"Point blank. It's the only way."

"I knew I never should have gone to Ikoden," Finaeus muttered. "I was just tempted by that famous salad place…."

Jessica checked the distance to Marsalla, and saw that the missiles would reach *Sabrina* ten seconds before they struck the planet's surface—on a plate fault line along the edge of a continent that Finaeus had selected.

"The instant the grapeshot fires, hit the stasis shields, Sabrina," Jessica ordered. "The explosions will mask us, and by the time it all clears, we'll be inside the planet."

<Yah, planetary camouflage, my favorite.>

"You got it, Sabrina?" Cargo asked.

<Of course, even if Jessica has the luckiest aim ever, we're still in the line of fire from relativistic shrapnel.>

Jessica saw Cargo nod, but not speak.

Her timer hit zero and the grapeshot fired. One RM exploded, but the other jinked aside, then back, and struck *Sabrina*—half a second after the stasis shields came online.

<Take that!> Sabrina cried out. *<My hide is thick! My armor is strong!>*

Sabrina collided with the planet.

One instant Sabrina had been crowing in delight and the next, Scan showed nothing but heat and pressure outside the stasis shield.

"How long!" Cargo called out.

<We were in full stasis for thirty seconds,> Sabrina replied. *<At best guess…judging by the pressure…we're thirty kilometers beneath the planet's surface.>*

"Max burn," Cheeky called out. "Antimatter is dry, spooling the nozzle back in. Using grav fields to give us a pocket for thrust."

The ship shuddered as the fusion engines slammed their energy into the magma surrounding the ship, slowing their downward momentum, then pushing them back toward the surface.

<This is surreal…and terrifying…> Sabrina said. *<SC Batt #3 is dry, Batt #2 is at eight percent and dropping fast.>*

"Nance?" Cargo asked. "What about the reactors."

<I'm shutting number one down. It almost went critical from the surge after full stasis. Two is running hot, but I can keep it going like this for another minute or so.>

"Then we have fifty-five seconds with this heat and pressure," Finaeus said. "Give or take a bit."

"No sweat," Cheeky said. "I'll have us out of here in fifty, easy."

Jessica didn't want to know what would happen when they reached the surface of the planet—which was likely molten for some distance—and their reactors and batts ran out of power.

No one spoke as the ship continued to shudder its way out of the magma, until—at precisely the time Cheeky had predicted—they burst free into the atmosphere.

The surface of Marsalla was a roiling ocean of magma and scattered remains of solid crust. Smoke and ash filled the air as Cheeky pulled the ship into a slow ascent.

"Stay low," Finaeus said. "Then come out at…thirty degrees, that should be in line with most of the debris flying out into space."

"*You* wanna fly?" Cheeky asked with a laugh. "I got this."

<*We're going to lose stasis shields in twenty seconds,*> Nance said. <*Try not to run into anything—we'll just have conventional shields, and point defense beams are on internal batteries only.*>

Cheeky slowly pulled *Sabrina* out of the atmosphere, until they had reached breakaway velocity, then she cut the engines.

Below them, Marsalla was in ruins. Cheeky had hit the fault line between where two major plates met, and the result was a supervolcano over a thousand kilometers across. Beyond the immediate ruin, tsunamis raced across the surface of the world, followed by ash and fire as more of the tectonic plates shifted and volcanic eruptions appeared along every fault line.

"The shockwave will shatter the far side of the planet," Finaeus said. "It'll be worse than this."

"Do this sort of thing often?" Cargo asked.

"Yeah, actually…. Though, not with ships I'm inside of at the time, but otherwise, yes, dozens of times."

"Oh."

"There's no way they'll see us," Jessica said. "We're actually going to pull this off…and we got a handy new ship to go with it."

"Can you get us on a vector to scoop from the star? I bet we can just slip by with our ramscoop out and pick up some fuel. No one will be looking for us?" Cargo said to Cheeky.

"Yeah, shouldn't be a problem. Will just take some small adjustments. I don't want to boost for a day or so, though. If we just drift on out for a few million klicks first that'll do nicely."

Jessica laughed. "Man, I wonder what they're thinking up on the station right now?"

"Nothing good." Cargo smiled. "Though they will get to terraform that planet for terrestrial life now."

"Let's hope," Finaeus said. "Though one thing is for certain. No one is doing anything there anytime soon."

OUTSYSTEM

STELLAR DATE: 09.04.8938 (Adjusted Years)
LOCATION: Hermes Station
REGION: Naga System, Orion Freedom Alliance Space

"OK, I suppose you're safe," Nance said as she pulled the hood off her hazsuit. "Iris was right. Those relatively-competent mad scientists bound the microbes to your skin so that the little nasties won't get free. Even if they did, they seem to have adapted to the polymers in such a fashion that the microbes would probably die if they were removed from their new environment."

"See," Jessica said, letting her skin glow a little more. "I told you I was perfectly safe. Glad I don't have to remove it either, I've grown rather attached to my glowing friends. Did I tell you I can stop a pulse blast with my hand?"

Nance sighed. "Yes, Jessica, just a few times now…like eight, or nine."

<*Ten, at least,*> Sabrina added.

Jessica slid off the medbay's examination table and pulled her shipsuit back on. "Yeah, well, it's really cool. It bears repeating."

<*I have stasis shields,*> Sabrina replied. <*I can smash into planets and destroy them. Stopping pulse blasts doesn't really compare.*>

"Touché," Jessica said with a laugh. "However, I'm Retyna Girl. You'll never take that from me."

<*And I'm 'Sabrina, Destroyer of Worlds'.*>

"Was she always so much into oneupmanship?" Jessica asked.

Nance chuckled. "More or less, yeah."

Jessica pulled on her shoes and jacket before approaching Nance.

"What are you doing?" Nance asked as she backed up.

"I want to give you a hug to thank you. You did some amazing work back there. Hacking the door to get *Sabrina* free, getting that nuke altered just in time. Keeping our skins on with power till we got free. Besides, you're still wearing your hazsuit."

"Your thanks is enough, you're not hugging me. Over my dead bo—"

Nance stopped talking as Jessica leapt forward and wrapped her in a tight embrace.

"Had to touch me eventually," Jessica said with a laugh as she stepped back.

"No, I didn't," Nance said. "Now I have to sanitize this suit."

"Seriously?" Jessica asked with a grin.

Nance's sour face held for a moment, and then she sighed and gave a small smile. "No, not seriously. But I have a reputation to uphold! Next time I tell you to stay in your EV suit, you stay in it!"

"Yes, Mom."

"What's with the 'Mom' stuff lately?"

*****

"So, have we selected a destination yet?" Jessica asked as she walked onto the bridge and took a seat at her console.

"There's a place called Kidron that looks pretty good," Cargo said. "It's better than the other options we were considering. A lot of mining rigs far out around the edges of the system. We can get in, do a bit of trading, get some more volatiles and get out fast."

"Just about ready to deploy the scoop, too," Cheeky said. "No indication that the locals have spotted us, either."

<*I'm but dust on the wind,*> Sabrina said in a sing-song voice.

"Think they'll pick up the scoop?" Jessica asked.

"If they have probes nearby looking straight at us, maybe," Cheeky said. "But really, we're kissing the star here. They're not going to see anything but star."

"Oh," Jessica said. "Once we're past the star…no one come into the rear observation lounge for a bit, kay?"

"Oh yeah?" Cheeky asked with an arched eyebrow.

"Yeah," Jessica replied. "I need some me time…well, me and Trevor time."

"In the sunlight."

"Oh, will that room be in full, ridiculously amazing sunlight?" Jessica asked.

Cargo sighed and shook his head. "What am I ever going to do with you two?"

* * * * *

"Deploying the scoop," Mandy announced.

"This is bullshit," Jenn said as she adjusted the ship's shielding to allow the ramscoop to draw in hydrogen and helium as they flowed off the star. "I can't believe we got kicked off Hermes of all places…and all because of that little shit Misha."

"Well…" Mandy chuckled. "He got his. Boarded a ship full of nut jobs that slammed themselves into a planet."

"I've never seen anything like that," Jenn replied. "What would possess them to do that? And how did they avoid those RMs?"

"I bet RHY is asking the same thing. Either way, no one is coming back to Naga anytime soon. This system's done."

"That's for sure," Jenn said.

Mandy studied scan, watching for potential flares and CMEs as they boosted past the star on a slingshot for the Jushes jump point.

"Whoa, what is that?" she asked.

"What is what?" Jenn said.

"There's another ship ahead, a few light seconds, just passing beyond scooping range," Mandy said. "I'm pulling up its pro—holy shit," she whispered the last two words.

"What?"

Mandy put the scan result on the small holodisplay between their seats.

"It's them," she said.

"The fuck! It *is* them."

"But they hit the planet," Mandy said. "Everyone in the system saw them hit Marsalla and smash it like a rotten egg."

"Well, then what are they doing on an outsystem vector?" Jenn asked.

"A vector too…Kidron!" Mandy locked eyes with Jenn.

"Mandy…we're not exactly welcome at a lot of places in Kidron."

"You willing to let Misha go—or a ship that can do what that one did?" She paused, her eyes widening as a grin spread on the face. "At the least we can sell the intel."

Jenn flipped her long braid over her shoulder and ran her fingers down its length for a minute. "OK, but just to sell the intel. I bet Derick would pay top dollar to know about a ship like that."

Mandy grinned and nodded. "Top dollar."

THE END

* * * * * *

Jessica and the crew of *Sabrina* have a long road ahead, and threats loom that they could only imagine. Their mission in the Naga system has not yielded them all the supplies they'll need, and maintaining the fiction of a trader will take some work.

Of course, no one would have anticipated that their subterfuge would involve a gala event: ***The Dance on the Moons of Serenity***.

THE BOOKS OF AEON 14

Keep up to date with what is releasing in Aeon 14 with the free Aeon 14 Reading Guide.

Origins of Destiny (The Age of Terra)
- Prequel: Storming the Norse Wind
- Book 1: Shore Leave (in Galactic Genesis until Sept 2018)
- Book 2: Operative (Summer 2018)
- Book 3: Blackest Night (Summer 2018)

The Intrepid Saga (The Age of Terra)
- Book 1: Outsystem
- Book 2: A Path in the Darkness
- Book 3: Building Victoria

- The Intrepid Saga Omnibus – *Also contains Destiny Lost, book 1 of the Orion War series*

- Destiny Rising – *Special Author's Extended Edition comprised of both Outsystem and A Path in the Darkness with over 100 pages of new content.*

The Orion War
- Book 1: Destiny Lost
- Book 2: New Canaan
- Book 3: Orion Rising
- Book 4: The Scipio Alliance
- Book 5: Attack on Thebes
- Book 6: War on a Thousand Fronts
- Book 7: Fallen Empire (2018)
- Book 8: Airtha Ascendancy (2018)
- Book 9: The Orion Front (2018)
- Book 10: Starfire (2019)
- Book 11: Race Across Time (2019)
- Book 12: Return to Sol (2019)

Tales of the Orion War
- Book 1: Set the Galaxy on Fire
- Book 2: Ignite the Stars
- Book 3: Burn the Galaxy to Ash (2018)

Perilous Alliance (Age of the Orion War – w/Chris J. Pike)
- Book 1: Close Proximity
- Book 2: Strike Vector
- Book 3: Collision Course
- Book 4: Impact Imminent
- Book 5: Critical Inertia (Sept 2018)

Rika's Marauders (Age of the Orion War)
- Prequel: Rika Mechanized
- Book 1: Rika Outcast
- Book 2: Rika Redeemed
- Book 3: Rika Triumphant
- Book 4: Rika Commander
- Book 5: Rika Infiltrator
- Book 6: Rika Unleashed (2018)
- Book 7: Rika Conqueror (2019)

Perseus Gate (Age of the Orion War)
Season 1: Orion Space
- Episode 1: The Gate at the Grey Wolf Star
- Episode 2: The World at the Edge of Space
- Episode 3: The Dance on the Moons of Serenity
- Episode 4: The Last Bastion of Star City
- Episode 5: The Toll Road Between the Stars
- Episode 6: The Final Stroll on Perseus's Arm
- Eps 1-3 Omnibus: The Trail Through the Stars
- Eps 4-6 Omnibus: The Path Amongst the Clouds

Season 2: Inner Stars
- Episode 1: A Meeting of Bodies and Minds
- Episode 3: A Deception and a Promise Kept
- Episode 3: A Surreptitious Rescue of Friends and Foes (2018)

- Episode 4: A Trial and the Tribulations (2018)
- Episode 5: A Deal and a True Story Told (2018)
- Episode 6: A New Empire and An Old Ally (2018)

Season 3: AI Empire
- Episode 1: Restitution and Recompense (2019)
- Five more episodes following...

The Warlord (Before the Age of the Orion War)
- Book 1: The Woman Without a World
- Book 2: The Woman Who Seized an Empire
- Book 3: The Woman Who Lost Everything

The Sentience Wars: Origins (Age of the Sentience Wars – w/James S. Aaron)
- Book 1: Lyssa's Dream
- Book 2: Lyssa's Run
- Book 3: Lyssa's Flight
- Book 4: Lyssa's Call
- Book 5: Lyssa's Flame

Legends of the Sentience Wars (Age of the Sentience Wars – w/James S. Aaron)
- Volume 1: The Proteus Bridge (August 2018)

Enfield Genesis (Age of the Sentience Wars – w/Lisa Richman)
- Book 1: Alpha Centauri
- Book 2: Proxima Centauri (2018)

Hand's Assassin (Age of the Orion War – w/T.G. Ayer)
- Book 1: Death Dealer
- Book 2: Death Mark (August 2018)

Machete System Bounty Hunter (Age of the Orion War – w/Zen DiPietro)
- Book 1: Hired Gun
- Book 2: Gunning for Trouble
- Book 3: With Guns Blazing

Vexa Legacy (Age of the FTL Wars – w/Andrew Gates)
- Book 1: Seas of the Red Star

Building New Canaan (Age of the Orion War – w/J.J. Green)
- Book 1: Carthage
- Book 2: Tyre (2018)

Fennington Station Murder Mysteries (Age of the Orion War)
- Book 1: Whole Latte Death (w/Chris J. Pike)
- Book 2: Cocoa Crush (w/Chris J. Pike)

The Empire (Age of the Orion War)
- The Empress and the Ambassador (2018)
- Consort of the Scorpion Empress (2018)
- By the Empress's Command (2018)

The Sol Dissolution (The Age of Terra)
- Book 1: Venusian Uprising (2018)
- Book 2: Scattered Disk (2018)
- Book 3: Jovian Offensive (2019)
- Book 4: Fall of Terra (2019)

ABOUT THE AUTHOR

Michael Cooper likes to think of himself as a jack of all trades (and hopes to become master of a few). When not writing, he can be found writing software, working in his shop at his latest carpentry project, or likely reading a book.

He shares his home with a precocious young girl, his wonderful wife (who also writes), two cats, a never-ending list of things he would like to build, and ideas...

Find out what's coming next at www.aeon14.com

Made in the USA
San Bernardino, CA
03 November 2018